A.K. KOONCE & HARPER WYLDE

HELL
KISSED

A.K. KOONCE & HARPER WYLDE

HELL
KISSED

To Sophie!

[signature]

Chapter One

Group Project

Rhys

"You're special, Rhys. Keep your head down. And know that you are love—"

The woman's eerie whisper changes abruptly into a harsh, blaring alarm that snaps my eyes wide open.

"Fuck," I hiss as I snuggle deeper down into the warmth of my blanket.

It's my first word of the day. Just like yesterday. And the day before. Then my dream and the hypnotic voice of the mysterious woman fades all too quickly from my mind as more terrifying thoughts shove in and stake their claim.

I have to partner with Kyvain and the other alpha fur-holes for our project in Speech 102. They'll make my life miserable for approximately forty-five minutes. That's not... too long. I can handle forty-five minutes.

It's a terrible way to start my morning, but...

"Shut that alarm off!" Mary yells from the kitchen.

My hand sneaks out from the blankets, and a cold chill races up my exposed flesh just long enough for me to hit the off button on the old alarm clock. I slink further into the warmth of my bedding and dwell on the day to come.

"Get your ass up, Rhys! I'm not going to hear another phone call from our alpha saying you're skipping classes again."

My eyes roll so far back that I think I just learned telepathy in a hidden part of my brain.

"For the last time, I didn't skip. Kyvain slammed his locker into my face, and I literally lost consciousness!" I mutter from under the safety of my blanket, fingers tracing the faint remains of the bruise that rings my eye from the incident. It still aches, but it's worlds better than it was a few days ago. My makeup will easily cover the faded blues and purples, erasing any evidence that he ever hurt me.

"Up!" she commands, and the moon mark across my chest burns instantly.

And I stand just as fast.

My jaw grinds, and I wish like hell I had a different relationship with my adoptive mother. She's been all I've known since I was seven. I don't really remember much before that except a blur of foster homes I never

belonged in. After all this time, Mary should be like a genuine mother to me, but she's never given me the affection a mother should.

She isn't at all like Bea's mom. Bea's my only friend, so her family is the only real example I have of what a family is supposed to be like.

And Mary, she should have adopted a stray dog instead of a child.

I saunter through my room and grab my clothes for the day. My project in speech keeps picking at the back of my mind, but I swallow it down and try to ignore it. I'm twenty-one years old. I'm too old to be afraid of some boy whose massive ego is probably making up for the shriveled little thing in his pants.

A warm caress flits across my calf, and I peer down at my number one fan in life.

"Aww, Loki," I say in that baby talk voice that even I hate.

The sweet little gray cat swishes his fluffy tail even more against my lower leg.

"Good morning, Loki," I say again with duck lips and all, fully understanding how ridiculous I look.

His meow is loud and demanding.

Right. Food.

Got it.

He's my number one fan because I am the goddess of food in his life. It feels a little like he's using me in that sense, but I'll take what I can get.

I fill his bowl near my door and slip out into the kitchenette. The smell of coffee is strong, and the deep frown on Mary's face is even stronger. Lines etch her tan features. Streaks of silver are smoothed back against her light brown hair, gathering into a loose bun that she wears nearly every day. She doesn't say anything or glance my way when I walk through the small room and into the bathroom to change and get ready.

I can't wait to move out, but in the Dark Moon Pack, you live with your parents until your first shift or until you're mated, a day Mary has been waiting for longer than even I have. Literally, our calendar has big red X's slashed across dates leading up to today. She hasn't acknowledged it or congratulated me, so clearly tonight's shifting ceremony is an exciting celebration for her.

Not for me.

I take my time combing through my white blonde hair. It hangs in a long veil around my pale features. After I've brushed my teeth, dabbed on some concealer around my left eye, and pulled on my jeans and black tee-shirt, I'm finally out of time. Speech class awaits.

And so do the alpha wolves.

The front door to our tiny cottage closes behind Mary with a heavy slam. Pressure shoves into my chest as I slide on my sneakers and grab my black bookbag.

Maybe I'll get lucky. Maybe I'll get another concussion in the hallway, and I won't even have to deal with the group project. Why is this an issue in my life? Why is my life so mundane that a group fucking project is the worst thing that could happen to me on the day of the Dark Moon?

Tension continues to build in my lungs and throat, but I refuse to think about it as I step out into the warm morning sunlight. It shines across my face in a calming ray of tranquility.

Everything's going to be fine.

Kyvain won't taunt me. And I won't accidentally attack his dick with my fist again.

Because *that* is truly the worst thing that could happen.

Alpha Morganson nearly disowned us that day. Mary was furious. She said we could easily be packless if I dishonored our alpha again. A lone wolf can't survive in the wild, she said. The *wild* being typical suburban America.

Shudder.

But she's right. I barely fit in with my own kind. How could I possibly live in the human world outside of our pack community in the quietest part of Los Angeles?

"Rhys!" Her excited voice blooms in my chest, and I can't explain the tingle of wolf magic that shakes through me.

"Bea!" I smile hard as she jogs from her cottage just next door to mine.

Her thick brown hair falls in glossy waves around bright green eyes. She's as beautiful as she is kind. The Dark Moon Celebration will be the night of her dreams, I'm sure.

She'll shift and find a mate. Me... I'll be lucky if

the brooding wolf inside me decides to show her face to this pack of assholes.

A man catches my attention from just behind Bea though. I freeze in my steps. He's a stranger. I've never seen him in our pack, I'm sure of it. Messy dark hair falls into his eyes as he follows my friend's movements until she gets to me. My heart stutters when I meet his intense, studious stare.

I blink, and the scent of ash singes the air.

Then he's gone.

I close my eyes and check again several times…

It's so busy out this morning, maybe it was just another neighbor with a bad hair day… bad hair *month*… year.

All around us, the other cottages are a rhythm of opening and closing doors. The community is more of a village. I've seen a human television in the mall that once referred to our pack as a cult during a news report.

They're not entirely wrong.

Take tonight for example. The entire pack is going to gather on the hill for the most important night of my entire life. The night of my twenty-first Dark Moon.

My wolf will finally show herself. Some will claim mates tonight, others will simply find themselves.

I'll probably be the latter… Maybe. If the she-wolf inside me feels like it. Because let's face it, she wears the pants in our relationship.

She's the alpha dom and I'm just some quiet

submissive who owns the body she struts around in.

I grimace at that thought but keep heading to the end of the lane where the monstrosity that is Dark Moon Community College awaits.

Our alpha's great-great-great-grandfather built the school himself. That explains why it's all one level and the windows slant on the left, like the institute had a bad stroke once upon a time.

"I'm paired up with Jov today," Bea whispers with a deep blush as we walk up the two small steps to the front entrance.

I bump my arm into hers and give her that smile I've always shown her when she mentions her crush. She's also paired with Monica and Aimee, but I guess she's forgetting those two narcissistic she-howlers. Thank God the teacher didn't pair me with Kyvain *and* those two.

We turn into the second room on the left, and the small speech class is filled with students who mill around before the lecture starts. I take a seat at the large table in the back, and Bea joins me there. The two seats on the other side of us remain empty.

I don't know why she does it. Why does she remain my friend when it doesn't gain her any brownie points with anyone else? Everyone loves Bea. She's the sweetest person I've ever met, and she's been my best friend for as long as I can remember.

I'm forever thankful that out of all the people in this place, she's my neighbor.

The scraping of a chair sounds near us, and I look up to find Jov pulling a chair over to Bea's side.

"Hey," he whispers with a shy smile.

"Hey," she says back in a breathy voice.

God. Stop it and ask her out already! Put her breathy, blushing girl brain out of its misery already, Jov!

That faint stirring swirls inside me once more, and I feel that magic even though I don't understand it. She's always there with me even though we've never met.

My wolf.

"Do you want to go to the Dark Moon with me tonight?" Jov blurts his question out, and even I'm impressed as I pretend to ignore the two lovesick puppies at my side.

"Oh. Yeah. That sounds great," Bea says with a smile eating up her words.

Wow. Way to go, Jov.

Really, it's a terrible idea. What if she mates with Benn or Calvin or one of the dozens of other men who check Bea out weekly?

Jov finally manned up and asked her on a date on the same night she might find her fated love. She might go with him and leave with someone else.

What an idiot.

He should have kissed her a long time ago, because tonight it might be too late.

He should have kissed her like she's always wanted...

A collective gasp and a moan of... *Why does that sound like a porn moan right now?*

I peek over out of the corner of my eye to find Bea's fingers threaded tightly through Jov's hair as he kisses her so hard even my own vagina is starting to get secondhand turned on right now.

Um…

"Mr. Ravensen, please remove yourself from Miss Stevens' tongue and find a different seat." Professor Reed stares at the couple down his thick-rimmed glasses, and it honestly takes several more lip locking kisses for the pair to separate.

Seriously. Kudos, Jov. What romance novel have you been reading to make a move like that?

Jov looks like he's in a daze as he stumbles over to the chair at the table across from us. And if I thought Bea was a blushing mess before…

She looks at me with the biggest smile, and I can't help but laugh.

Damn.

Who knew Jov Ravensen was a dream man?

Mr. Reed flips through the calendar on his desk at the front of the room and the class quiets, despite several girls throwing curious glances at Jov and Bea.

"Everyone pair up with your assigned groups. Your debate on Pack Origins: Blessed by the Gods or an Evolutionary Trait, is due by the end of the week." The professor plops down in a black swivel chair behind his paper cluttered desk and seems set on ignoring us all for the next forty-five minutes.

My heart slams and dips down hard as I lift my chin and look up at the man seated two tables ahead of me. Calvin slouches down in the seat across from Kyvain with a twisted smile kissing his lips. Calvin tosses his bag into the chair next to him as he speaks quickly and quietly. I can't see anything but Kyvain's unruly blond hair and arrogant square shoulders.

I stand slowly, and as I walk to their table, a mantra of good vibes and calming energy circles my mind.

Don't punch him in the dick. Don't punch him in the dick. Don't punch him in the dick.

My sneakers squeak when I stop at the empty chair at Kyvain's side. Without a word, I lower my bag to the table, but his hand flies out fast. He shoves the bookbag from the surface, and it hits the old tile floor with a solid thud.

"Seat's taken. Sorry, Rice," he says with a cruel smirk on his lips as he mispronounces my name like we haven't been in school together since second grade. His fingers tap the desktop, his large family ring glinting like a constant reminder of his status in our pack.

The wolf in me stirs. That's truly our problem... *my* problem. I'm no different than any other girl in this pack, but my wolf is. And they know it. The beasts in them recognize the beast in me, and for some reason she isn't like the others. She doesn't bow to social norms. She doesn't care about respect or alphas.

She will fuck Kyvain's perfect little egotistical world up. And she doesn't give a shit that I suffer her consequences.

Maybe that will change with time. Maybe once she

and I bond tonight, I'll no longer be a target for assholes like Kyvain.

"There are only three of us." I try not to roll my eyes, but the chair next to Calvin has two backpacks slouched in it, and it's becoming very obvious that they've intentionally waited for me to take this seat.

Or try to, at least.

"Seat's taken. I don't know what you want me to do about it." His striking blue eyes that are so similar to his father's look up at me.

I don't look around. I don't dare let him think he's as superior as he acts.

Even if he really is.

There are two shoving, conflicting emotions warring inside me. One is my own—that's the nervous side.

And the other… the other is the wolf who likes to get me in trouble. That's the I'll-kick-your-ass-and-I-don't-give-a-fuck-what-your-daddy-has-to-say-about-it side.

My wolf didn't get the memo about us possibly being rejected from the pack who took us in out of the kindness of their hearts. No, she doesn't give a wolf's furry ass about rejection.

"Do you want me to move the chair to the other side?" I suggest with a sugary sweetness I don't feel, striving to be the good little peacemaker I know I should be.

"No." Kyvain shakes his head slowly, a ruthless glint in his blue gaze. "You know what I want, Rice-a-

Roni." He nods to the right, but… nothing's there. Just an empty aisle between work desks.

I shrug, confusion pulling at my brows.

What. Does. He. Want? Just get it over with already!

"Be a good girl and *sit*," he says with a sharp curve of his lips.

Calvin snorts under his breath, and it dawns on me that Kyvain wants me to sit on the floor at his side.

Like a dog. Like the whore he often calls me.

A current of anger rises up, and a growl hums at the back of my mind as I stare at the asshole in front of me.

"Sit," he hisses once more, the air of alpha authority he likes to lord over me filling his harsh command. Someday, he'll probably take over his father's position and lead the pack. What will happen to me then?

My heartbeat thrashes, and that nervous, kind side of me that I cling to so hard is quickly stomped over by the wolf that hides deep inside. She refuses to obey, and the demand he expects me to follow rolls off my shoulders like water as I ignore him.

His eyes flash for the direct slight, and I can practically feel his own wolf bristle and snarl at the insubordination.

Fuck him.

"It's sad really," I say without thinking.

"What is?" Kyvain snaps.

"That tiny dick syndrome causes so much

12

aggression in men like yourself." Sometimes I surprise myself with my bravado, but ages of being bullied will do that to a person.

All the snarky replies I've built up over the years wait on my tongue like an arsenal, ready to be used when they push me far enough. It doesn't take much for my wolf's rage and my own smart mouth to get there these days. The closer I get to the Dark Moon, the closer my wolf seems to be, and the thinner my self-preservation filter becomes.

Kyvain's chair slams back so fast, it clatters to the floor with a racket of noise that draws every single set of eyes to the two of us. He stares me down like an alpha ready to attack. I should bow out. I should look away. I should lower my head to my future alpha.

Instead, my chin lifts higher.

"Is there a problem, Mr. Morganson?" Professor Reed asks slowly, his beady eyes shifting from the golden boy alpha to the outcast that I am.

Nervousness spikes through me, sending a million butterflies loose in a torrent of anxiety, while Kyvain's furious blue eyes slice me into tiny, insignificant pieces.

"Not at all," Kyvain finally says. It seems he physically puts thought into placing a charming smile on his lips when he looks up at our professor. "Rhys was just saying she wasn't feeling well. Might have to go home. She might even have to skip the Dark Moon Celebration tonight. If she knew what was good for her, that is." He holds that subtle threat over me.

I stand in the middle of the class with all eyes on

me.

With a thick clearing of his throat, Professor Reed meets my lost expression. "I think he's right. You should head home for the day. Get your rest, Miss Love."

Calvin snickers quietly.

Bea looks up at me with big, sad eyes.

And Kyvain, he doesn't give me a second glance now that he's dismissed me like he owns me.

What if my entire life is like this?

What if my entire existence is one big, dreaded group project?

I'll never survive it.

Chapter Two

The Stranger

Rhys

A cool breeze ruffles my light blonde hair, and I tuck it back as I make my way down the sidewalk toward the small two-bedroom house that barely resembles the word 'home.' The outside looks cozy enough with its blue door and shutters, and the yellow flowers dotting the garden on either side of the small front stoop, but I have to admit to myself that these four walls have always felt temporary.

I kick my white sneaker at the smooth pavement just outside my cottage. Mary is going to be mega pissed if she finds out I came home early. Thankfully she's still working at the lab in town, and I won't see her until tonight at the celebration.

If I go…

The wolf within me snarls.

I guess I might go...

Then another snapping of teeth.

Fucking fine, we'll go!

A happy warmth spreads through me, and I roll my eyes at the demanding bitch.

I pull my house key from my bookbag, and when I look up, he's there again. Stormy eyes bore into mine, searching for something I'm not sure he finds. The stranger stands at the corner of my little cottage, and it seems odd that the warm magic inside me spreads even more at the creepy sight of a strange man watching me.

Jesus, Kyvain has seriously fucked with my ability to rationally remember fight or flight in times like this.

Hesitantly, I look around at my surroundings. The elderly woman across the street, Mrs. Linskey, is tending to her roses out front. Mr. Brooks is mowing his lawn just two houses down.

This is my pack.

I'm safe here.

Then who the fuck is this guy?

"Can I help you?" I ask stiffly, holding my key more like a weapon now. The security of the jagged metal only comforts me a little, but at least I have a way to defend myself if needed.

He looks over his shoulder at the woman gardening and then to the man mowing. He's calculating, almost like he's debating if they'd come to my rescue if he moved any closer. To be honest, I don't know the answer. The elders here are a bit kinder. Mostly, though, the pack tolerates me. I'm definitely the lowest member of the pack hierarchy, at least until tonight. Maybe my first shift will change everything. Or maybe my defiant wolf will condemn me to live the same torturous cycle on repeat.

His attention flicks back to me from beneath thick, black lashes. Then he shakes his head.

And bursts into fucking flames.

A scream rips from my throat. He disappears with the scent of ash clinging to the breeze. My wide eyes search him out, but he's gone.

And I've been traumatized for life.

***

I rest. Or at least I try to.

Kyvain was being a furry fuckwad, but I think he was right, I do need rest, because I am seeing some unexplainable shit today.

He was there! He… he definitely was.

Maybe I should call Mary about the strange guy outside. But she hates it when I call her at work.

Bea will be home in an hour.

I roll onto my side, my fingers still gripping my keys hard in my hand beneath the blue blanket, unable to let them go. A soft purring is the only sound in the house, and trust me, I have listened to every little creak of the foundation at this point. I close my eyes slowly and try not to think about the burning man, but the image of his dark features behind the flickering flames as he inexplicably disappeared is hard to forget. It's seared in my memory like a scene from a bad horror movie.

Just relax. You'll go next door in an hour and you'll be fine.

Everything will be fine.

"Everything will be fine, Rhys," the far-off woman whispers as my eyes grow heavy and my mind drifts. "You're special, but you can't stay here. Everything will be fine for a little while."

The lullaby of her words swirl in my thoughts. It's the most calming tone, and yet, it pricks at my mind like a sharp needle the more and more she speaks.

"Always remember that you are love—"

My eyes flash open and darkness blankets my room. Pale white moonlight peeks in through my window.

The moon!

I throw the blankets off in a swoosh of movement. My messy hair is tangled around my face, and I shove it all back as I stumble to get my shoes on.

Fuck. Fuck. Fuck!

A meowing screech hisses through the room as I trip over something tragically fluffy.

"Shit! I'm sorry, Loki!"

"You named your cat Loki?" a dark, rumbling whisper seeps through the room.

This time when I stumble, my back hits the wall hard, and my ass slams against the floor even harder.

"What the fuck?" I hold my key firmly out between myself and the shadow of a man leaning

against my bedroom wall, wielding the metal like it's a deadly sword instead of the pathetic weapon it truly is.

"W-What do you want?"

"Why the hell did you name your cat after a cruel god?" A hypnotic accent caresses his words as he saunters closer, like a nightmare stalking right into my life.

My thoughts tumble through my mind one after another, and why the hell he cares so much about my cat is suddenly at the top of the pile.

"And why is your blade so tiny?" He lowers himself until he's kneeling just before me, looking curiously at the key in my hand.

"It's a key," I whisper on a shaking breath.

"Huh," is all he says as he pokes at it with the tip of his pointer finger

"Not very… stabby." His brows pull low over starlit blue eyes. "Have you ever considered one of these?" He stands, and with a turn of his hand, a beam of fire erupts, slashing out fast before sizzling into a long iron blade.

My gasp catches in my throat, unable to escape as my eyes widen.

The wolf in me warms, impressed and amazed like this man is now my own personal party magician instead of a stalker and possible killer. The drilling of my heartbeat is the only logical sign that I know I should run. But he's just too close. He could slice my head clean off before I even made it a single step.

For self-preservation, I decide to stay where I am.

On the floor.

"What do you want?" I ask again in a steady but breathless tone.

His attention flits back to me like he momentarily forgot the cowering woman he was holding hostage in the corner of the room. There's a shift in his stance. Ashen boots pace shortly before he looks to me once more.

"The girl this morning. She's your friend?"

Thoughts spin wildly in my mind.

This is about Bea?

What does this asshole want with Bea? A growl creeps up from the back of my mind and slips past my lips.

"I mean… you have friends here. A caregiver too. I saw the woman who left early this morning, and then your friend came right out to meet you. You're loved here?"

Sudden laughter that I can't stop bursts out of me, the sound is sharp with a sarcastic edge.

"Oh my God," I gasp with a smile I can't contain. "Literally no one has ever said that to me." I try to reel in my crazy girl hysteria, but it just dissolves into the pathetic realization that he's so incredibly wrong. I couldn't stop the pang in my chest if my life depended on it.

Messy hair falls into his pretty eyes as he tilts his head at me in blank confusion. He turns his wrist quickly, and the weapon in his hand sparks brightly before turning to ash and dissolving entirely. The

remnants of it float through the moonlight, and my wide eyes follow the tiny particles of magic.

I've never seen magic like his before.

"I made a mistake." He turns away from me and heads toward the door. "She was wrong," he says quietly as a goodbye.

What does that mean?

My sneakers slip as I scramble to my feet. I'm right behind him in the darkness of the kitchen, but he just keeps going.

"Who? Who was wrong?"

He pulls open the door and pale moonlight streams across the worn tiles, reminding me that the Dark Moon won't wait for me. Still, I can't let this guy go without getting an explanation.

"Who?" I scream once more.

The mysterious man turns on his heel, his blue eyes sharp even in the growing shadows of the deepening night. Somehow, the darkness enhances their color, turning them into gleaming sapphires that cut through me with the intensity of a tidal wave.

"Your mother wanted me to tell you that you are loved." His deep, rich voice is like a bad omen that makes my heart drop instantly.

And with a heavy scent of ash, he bursts into flames, flickering out into drifting sparks that float into the starry night sky. I gape into the darkness where he once stood, staring after him with fear and want tangling tightly together in my chest.

He's gone. And so are the answers I suddenly need

now more than ever.

Chapter Three

Personal Space

Rhys

The sound of my sneakers thudding against the pavement almost matches the rapid beating of my heart as I run through town square to make it to the pack gathering at the edge of the woods.

My wolf huffs in dry amusement, and I know if she could pull off human expressions, she'd be arching one perfectly polished eyebrow at me.

Okay… running might be a liberal use of the word.

Her amusement turns downright judgmental.

Fuck, fine. Speed walking.

I'm trying here!

Either way, I hurry my ass off and hope I can slip

in unnoticed. If there's one thing Alpha Morganson hates, it's tardiness. He sees it as insubordination, and though I'm just a lowly wolf who he views as zero threat to his alpha status, being late will be as inexcusable of an offense as punching his son in that little thing he calls a dick. It doesn't matter that he deserved a small taste of the same medicine he dishes out daily.

Hurry, hurry, hurry! The mantra pushes me harder, fear of the alpha's wrath quickening my footsteps until I'm jogging. He won't care that I just had my life infiltrated by a tall, dark, and frustratingly mysterious stranger. I doubt he'd even believe the tale was true.

A coldness stings across my cheeks as I hustle faster. A chill hits my lungs. My attention lifts to the dark sky to find...

"It's snowing," I whisper, and stumble a step.

It was eighty degrees this morning. I've never even seen snow before. Not here. The Mountain Wolf Pack north of here has spoken of it, but...

"What's happening?" I try to keep moving. I try to ignore all the insane things that keep piling onto this day.

The road comes to an intersection, the college on the right and our market to the left. But the four way is closed off by nothing more than people traveling toward the woods.

No one will be using the roads tonight.

I swallow hard when I spot the fringes of the crowd on the hill. The whole pack seems to have gathered for the Dark Moon, but it makes sense. This is Kyvain's Dark Moon as well, and he demands nearly as much respect as his father, even at his young age.

Personally, I think it's ridiculous that a bunch of older wolves kiss his ass because he may be our next alpha. It's the most likely scenario, but all it does is inflate his already oversized ego. If it gets any bigger, people are going to have to start moving to the dreaded suburbs just to get some breathing room.

Dwelling on that douchebag is my least favorite pastime, but I welcome the mental break it gives me from thinking about the dark stranger who showed up perfectly prepared to wreck my life.

"Your mother wanted me to tell you that you are loved."

Those words still echo through my mind with every breath I pull into my lungs as I join the gathering crowd and catch my breath.

There is one thing I know with certainty.

He wasn't talking about Mary.

I'm not sure my adopted mother feels one ounce of affection for me. I'm no more than her assigned responsibility. Kyvain once told me our alpha made Mary take me in because she was the only widow in our pack without children. I know he was just taunting me, but it doesn't really sound like a lie. I know she's hoping to offload me tonight after my wolf appears.

She's going to be pissed if I come home tonight without a mate or a plan to move out.

But I'll have a plan. I'll move into the college dorms for the rest of the semester and then… I don't know. I don't know where I'm supposed to go in the world when it doesn't feel like there's a place for me in it.

The stranger's eerie words about my mother circle my mind.

I've always wondered about my birth parents, but my adoption was closed.

I've hoped that someday I'd learn who they were, but I gave up wishing they'd magically appear and save me from my shitty life.

Still… I can't help but wonder.

Is she looking for me? Is there a place for me? With her? I shake those thoughts away.

For now at least. Too many questions linger, but the biggest ones just won't fade. If she was alive, why did she give me up? And perhaps more importantly, what does she want with me now?

The woodland is shoulder to shoulder with every member of our pack out beneath the stars to celebrate this year's Dark Moon. The open space is lined with trees and plenty of room to run. Which is good for the wolves who will be ripping out into the world for the first time.

Mary leans against a tree, standing alone in her white lab coat as if she came right after work. Her gaze shifts over the crowd and she spots me. We lock eyes. She stares blatantly at me as if she's picking me apart where I stand.

And then she looks away. She shifts and fully turns her back on me.

"Hi to you too, Mom," I mumble to myself. My eyes roll, but the raging lover of violence inside of me snarls.

Calm down, I soothe the wolf.

She's a cunt. Not a threat.

Smiles and laughter flit through the night, and I'm so incredibly lucky nothing has started yet. A heavy breath pushes from my lips as I slip into the crowd unnoticed, until a hand complete with paper thin skin clutches my wrist.

A jolt of nerves spikes through me.

My neighbor, Mrs. Linskey, pulls me to a stop with surprising strength for an elderly lady. Her hands are so cold. She isn't dressed for the light snowfall tonight.

None of us are.

Brown eyes stare back at me with more clarity than I've ever seen in her eighty-three-year-old gaze.

"Are you okay, Mrs. Linskey?" I'm half afraid she's having a stroke.

She shouldn't be out here in the cold.

I'm partial to the sweet old woman who used to bake me cookies when the other kids in the neighborhood wouldn't play with me.

Other than my friendship with Bea, it's the only kindness I remember from my childhood. Unless providing basic food, shelter, and clothing counts. Then Mary would have to be added to that sparkling list.

Some asshole barrels past me, fully knocking me into Mrs. Linskey. I stagger. Afraid we're going to tumble to the ground together, I try to twist to the side so I don't take her down with me.

Surprisingly, her grip tightens, and I'm yanked forward until I'm steady on my feet.

A strange sensation presses against my chest. I study her closely, but she doesn't speak. There's no bright light of charisma in her eyes.

There's just emptiness.

The uneasy feeling within me spreads, but I try to just calm down after the asinine day I've had.

White eyebrows furrow on her face in a look of pure confusion.

Anxiously, I glance toward the gathering in time to see the festivities commencing. Alpha Morganson's rich voice bellows across the clearing, commanding everyone's attention.

I attack my bottom lip with my teeth, but my decision is already made.

"Why don't we find somewhere off to the side to sit?" I offer as another jerkwad rams their shoulder into my back to get a better view of what's going on up ahead. Like listening to a politician drone on is the highlight of their whole year. I glare perfectly ignorable daggers at the wolf who doesn't seem to care that he just branded my body with the bruise his shitty manners have surely left on my back. "This place is practically a mosh pit."

Mrs. Linskey stares at me like I'm a one thousand piece jigsaw puzzle she can't figure out. A wave of warmth washes over me—magic I can't ignore—and

I try to push it in her direction. I know my mysterious magic makes people feel good.

Her eyes widen, and I know she feels the unexplainable effects, even if she doesn't understand them.

Deafening cheers rise through the crowd at something Alpha Morganson said in the speech I'm not paying attention to.

Together, we glance toward the front of the gathering, but the last thing I need to hear is more endless commentary on how much this night means. As if there isn't enough pressure placed on our first shift.

I swear some of the other wolves in the vicinity are eyeing me with unfettered curiosity.

Fuck.

I'm stunned to hear two of them whispering and even exchanging money, waging bets on my shift. There are some who think I won't shift into a wolf at all, but some other creature entirely. Or perhaps they're wagering that my wolf will be even more defiant once she's released, taking bets on what punishment the alpha will inflict upon me first.

Or maybe, just like Mary, our alpha will be ready to push me from the pack I've known my entire life…

A sharp pain grinds out in the bones of my wrist as Mrs. Linskey's grip tightens. She's gazing around as surely as I am, noticing the same attention we're suddenly receiving.

"Come on." I nod toward the sidelines that

suddenly look much more appealing. Being the center of attention makes me uncomfortable. It means a fight is likely to occur. And the elderly shouldn't be in the middle of that. The old woman follows after me as I lead her away from the crowd and down one sloping side of the hill. "Let's get you out of here."

It doesn't escape my notice that my neighbor hasn't uttered a single word, and the concern about the stroke she could be having comes roaring back right as a warmth I can't explain spreads through my chest like the slow burning of a fire in winter air. It creeps through me like spreading ink until it covers every surface, thoroughly distracting me.

My wolf perks up.

And I slam into a slab of steel.

Air rushes from my lungs in a whoosh. They burn for more oxygen which I scramble to give them until large hands clamp down on my shoulders, stealing my breath entirely. The scent of fire mixes with something sharper that I can't define.

All I know is that cologne companies would make a killing if they bottled the fragrance.

My gaze traces the defined lines of a tee-shirt clad chest until I'm staring into the hard russet eyes of the most sinfully scary man I've ever seen in my life.

There's something about dangerous men that gives them an allure I may never understand. His attraction is like a rush of adrenaline. Like playing with fire.

In the midst of Hell.

Shadows play over his face, swirling like smoke. His eyes are the color of dying embers, the reddish brown of his gaze burning holes into me.

I half expect to bleed from the intensity of it.

He focuses on my face, his steadfast gaze tracing over my features, and for the second time today, I wonder if I'm slowly losing my grasp on reality.

"Who the fuck are you?" I pat myself on the back for keeping my voice serious and steady despite the rapid beating of my heart.

My question stands. I've never seen this guy in my life. There's no way I'd ever forget those eerie, otherworldly eyes.

"Don't tell me you didn't feel it." The bastard ignores me completely and speaks to Mrs. Linskey, who finally releases me.

I glance to the elderly woman and then back to the man who looks like a fucking mascot for the Irish mob.

"How do you know her?" I ask the deadly-looking stranger.

He passes a hard look from me to her. "I'm her fucking caretaker. Clearly."

"Can't even take care of your fucking self, asshole," Mrs. Linskey murmurs with a totally out of character eye roll and shake of her head.

What. The. Fuck?

I rub at the ache in my wrist, eyes flitting between the odd pair before me. Racking my brain, I try to remember if Mrs. Linskey has a family. She's always alone, but it's possible her family lives with another close pack in the mountains.

On the rare occasion I went into her home, I never paid attention to the picture frames cluttered on every surface, but it's possible this guy truly is her caretaker... a grandson maybe... who happens to enjoy biker gangs and fist fights on the weekends...

I study him openly. He's older than me. That much is clear, but it's easy to tell he's still in his twenties. There's a youthfulness to his skin despite the ruggedness of his features

Though his eyes dare me to guess again. Their stormy blaze alludes to a hardness most people don't experience in one lifetime, let alone twenty-eight or twenty-nine short years.

"It can't possibly be her," Mrs. Linskey says, though her voice is devoid of the typical aging grit. Each note sounds... off. The melody of it is all wrong. "This pack would much rather be rid of her. There's no *love* lost."

I blink. Did I... Did I hear that correctly? The words are a dagger to the heart, plunging deeply and twisting as one of my only allies condemns me.

I feel like I'm still dreaming, trapped in a nightmare. That would at least let me explain all the weird shit that's gone on today.

Hot flames burst out. A flicker of raging fire ignites over Mrs. Linskey, burning up her thin shawl and the flesh beneath. I choke on my scream as her skin ashes away and transforms into a tall man where she was just standing.

That… that's not possible!

The same guy who's been stalking me all day appears in her place as if it was the most natural occurrence in the world. A jagged breath trembles over my lips. I'm already retreating slowly, shaking my head like I've lost my damn mind.

No one will ever believe this.

They'll medicate me. They'll shut me away like I'm more of an embarrassment to the pack than I already am.

Though I have a million questions sitting on my tongue, my flight-or-fight response is firmly switched to run, and I nearly trip over my feet as I scramble backward over the light blanket of snow.

"Rhys," the one with the starlit blue eyes growls out, but I can't get away from the two men glaring at me fast enough. It's not lost on me that he knows my fucking name.

Wet grass slides beneath my shoes as I whip around quickly, only to run smack into yet another hard chest. What the fuck is with everyone getting in my way tonight? I'm rarely around people, and tonight I can barely walk without slamming into someone or being bumped into.

It's called personal space, people.

And I really fucking need it in the middle of a mental crises.

I rub my chest, cringing at the pain that blooms in my tit from the person I practically eradicated in my haste to get the fuck out of here.

My face barely rises before my gaze locks on Kyvain's ugly sneer. Because, of course, the universe really wants to ass fuck me today.

And I have zero time to react before he backhands me. The sting is worse against the chill in my cheeks.

Yeah.

I never should have gotten out of bed this morning.

Chapter Four

Imaginary Friends

Rhys

Copper floods my mouth as my head whips sideways with enough force to snap a human's neck. Good thing I'm a wolf, or Mary would be planning my funeral and collecting one or two sympathy cards by now.

I wonder if it matters to her if I leave her life with a moving truck or in a body bag. I tell myself she'd be sad, but the truth needles. She'd take a day or two to mourn my death before turning my bedroom into an office.

My wolf grumbles.

Yeah. Two days is probably too generous.

Calvin snickers at Kyvain's side and I palm my aching cheek. Part of me is shocked he hit me in public, and the other part is pissed.

"I thought my warning this morning was rather clear. You're not welcome here." Kyvain takes a menacing step forward, clearly hoping to intimidate me with his broad build, icy glare, and harsh rebuke.

Joke's on him.

He's not even the scariest monster I've encountered today, and I have zero fucks left to give.

My wolf hums happily, clearly pleased I'm finally putting her asshole personality to good use.

A quick glance behind me shows that I'm alone once again. And once more, I'm wondering if I imagined the entire encounter with the two strange men.

Fuck. Is it possible Kyvain found a way to drug me earlier?

It's the only option that remotely makes sense.

"The Dark Moon is for everyone, Kyvain," I reply, more than a little annoyed. "I'm going to shift whether you try to kick me out or not." I lift my chin toward the rising moon.

It's almost fully above us, and my skin practically tingles with the magic of my first shift. My wolf writhes under my skin, ready to break through for the first time and fully reveal herself.

Revenge isn't far from her mind. The desire to rip a hole in Kyvain and teach him a lesson rides me hard enough that I have to swallow and roll my neck to hold her back.

Warmth seeps over my stinging cheek and the pain morphs to a prickling that tells me I'll have yet another bruise. Luckily, as soon as I shift, I'll begin healing faster.

There's blood on my palm from a cut on my cheekbone, and I can only conclude it was put there by the signet ring Kyvain wears on his left hand. Their family crest is embossed in the surface of the gold. If he had punched me, I'd be wearing the symbol like a brand.

I grit my teeth as Kyvain's alpha authority sinks into me like poison.

"You crossed a line this morning, Rhys." Kyvain's chest practically brushes against mine as he menacingly invades my personal space. Fear trickles through the normal part of me, but it only gets so far, unable to penetrate the anger radiating from my wolf. "You shouldn't have opened that pretty little mouth of yours, but you'll be opening it on command for me real soon."

Kyvain exchanges a crude smile with Calvin, the twist of his lips a leer that's far too dangerous for his pretty face. As much as I hate him, I have to admit that he comes from a good set of genes. Unfortunately, he's far too ugly on the inside to be considered good-looking.

A biting smile tenses my lips as I lean in good and close to make sure he understands my quiet, rasping words.

"I guess no one's told you," I whisper innocently.

"You have to have a dick in order for someone to suck it." I pull back and flip him off before shouldering my way past the two of them.

The unyielding nerve of this asshole is astounding.

But fuck, does it feel good to give in to the wolf side of me.

Long fingers wrap around my bicep with bruising force before I've even made it a full step. Kyvain jerks me into the hard line of his body.

My stomach dips and rolls, riding a rollercoaster of its own making. Being this close to him is vomit inducing.

A growl rumbles through the darkness, but Kyvain and his crony don't seem to notice. Or maybe they don't hear it the way I do.

This is taking 'imaginary friends' a little too far. Just don't look at them.

They're not there. They're not there. There's no such thing as exploding men on fire…

Right?

I swallow, pissed off that I have no way to extract myself from Kyvain's grip. He's bigger and stronger than I am. My knee is about to meet his groin when his next words chill me to the fucking bone.

"It makes the news I get to deliver to you so much sweeter because you think your life is still your own," Kyvain rumbles darkly. "You belong to the pack, Rice." My shitty nickname flows off his tongue. He does it on purpose, but this time there's a promise hidden behind the way he says it.

An ownership.

Dread settles over my heart like a lead blanket. "Your mother is making arrangements right this minute with my father, bartering your life for a better one for herself. You won't get a mate. We all know it. You fucking know it. You'll be no better than a pack whore. And I get you to myself first."

He's lying. He is.

But still, doubt creeps in.

A million emotions fly through me, but I settle on anger. My wolf wants to snap her teeth and rip Kyvain's face off just to rid him of the smug satisfaction gleaming in his blue eyes. He thinks he's cornered me, but I'm no wilting flower.

My gaze shoots into his with the intensity of a high-powered laser.

"I'll never be your whore," I promise him right back and try to tear myself from his grasp.

"That's where you're wrong," he purrs, and the sound is more fear inducing than a snarl from our beasts. "You've always been a whore. Now we're just making it official. You're going to regret what you said about my dick when I leave you unable to walk in the morning."

He grabs my ass and hauls me against him so I can feel just how tiny his cock really is.

My throat constricts. Curving fingers squeeze too tightly. His breath is hot against my face. It suffocates me. I can't breathe.

A growl slashes through the darkness. This time,

Kyvain's eyes flick away from mine to search the shadows behind me. Icy tingles prick along my arms with the sense of danger.

"Aric." Though I can't see him, the warning bite comes from stalker number one. I'm already attuned to the warm, calming timbre of the burning man from earlier.

A darker, deeper voice answers out of thin air. "I'm going to Hell anyway. What can she do to me?"

Hell? She?

All questions I file away for later.

My lips curve into a knowing smile as I watch Kyvain's eyes widen as he takes in stalker number two, Aric, who emerges from the shadows as if he was bred from them.

"Don't. Don't do this," Stalker One warns, but Aric keeps prowling forward. "Or ignore me. Whatever," Stalker One mutters, but he does nothing to stop Aric from striding right up to Kyvain and wrapping a meaty hand around the alpha's throat. Tattoos decorate his arms in thick lines and intricate pictures I could spend hours studying. They disappear below the tee-shirt that molds itself against his body.

Kyvain releases me instantly, and I skirt sideways before looking around for the other magical man. There's nothing. The crowd is all gathered tightly up on the hill, oblivious to what's happening in the shadows below, and the burning man is nowhere to be seen.

Again.

He leaves me just as confused as I've been all day. In the distance, past the pack that always ignores my existence, I see Mary animatedly chatting with Alpha Morganson, and the vise around my heart tightens.

She wouldn't offer me as a whore… Alpha Morganson wouldn't allow it…

"Who… are… you?" Kyvain gasps with the limited air he's still able to breathe.

"I tried that question already," I sass with more bravado than I should probably feel. "Good luck getting anything more than cryptic riddles if you get any answer at all." My hands hit my hips, and just seeing Kyvain so weak empowers me more than ever.

Or perhaps that's the magic of the Dark Moon.

Calvin's Adam's apple bobs hard as he stares at his best friend with wide, scared shitless eyes. What a good little beta wolf. *Such a good boy.*

Honestly, I can't fully blame him. Aric is massive, far out bulking Kyvain and Calvin. There's no question who I'd put my money on to win a fight, and the beta knows it.

"You're trespassing on my territory." Kyvain's growl comes out as more of a squeak when Aric tightens his hold with a casual tensing of his long fingers.

If these eerie men plan to continue following me around, it's about time they made themselves useful. This is nice. I should have a harem of guards like this going forward. Hell, the two of them could be more than guards depending on their mood.

I wonder if stalker boy one is very good at fanning someone with an overly large tropical leaf...

I'm distracted when a slicing amusement cuts across my guard's cruel features. Aric's teeth are somehow sharper than normal, and his feral smile gleams in the pale moonlight.

Proving just how much of an idiot he truly is, Kyvain clearly dismisses every sign of danger. I guess it makes sense. His father raised him to believe he was invincible, the second strongest among us. The right hand to the alpha, an untouchable legacy.

A total. Fucking. Idiot.

"She belongs to me," Kyvain spits.

A cold, dry sound of disgust cuts through the shadowed night. "She belongs to no one," Aric growls.

My heart pitter-patters in my chest like a besotted schoolgirl's while I stare at the monster before me in complete and utter shock. No one ever stands up for me. Bea tried, but over time I've convinced her it isn't worth putting herself in the line of fire. I've always been the bullseye of the pack's bullying, particularly Kyvain's, and I never want to get her dragged into it.

Whatever beef they have is centered on me and the strangeness of my beast within.

Funny how Aric turned from stalker to savior in under a minute.

Is it possible to fall for a complete stranger? Because I think I just fucking fell in love with this murderous asshole.

"I'll have your head for this!" Kyvain bares his teeth, but it's a pathetic attempt to make himself seem more menacing. He's like a kitten left out in the rain at this point.

Aric's evil laughter skirts down my spine. Inch by inch he lifts Kyvain off the ground until he's kicking and flailing, scratching at the giant hand collared around his throat.

"Stronger men have tried. And in the end, I still feasted on their eyes like little cocktail weenies." The deadly man's threat is odd but honest, it seems.

"No one knows tiny cocktail weenies like Kyvain," I add, despite my grimace at the thought of what the psycho to my left just described.

A heavy thud resounds as Aric drops him in a heap at his feet. My classmate lies in the mud like a crumpled up wad of paper.

It's a good look for Kyvain. I like it.

My tormentor surges to his feet with death blazing in his eyes, but Aric doesn't even blink, let alone flinch. More danger radiates from Aric's adorably tattooed pinkie than Kyvain's entire body.

Calvin's chest is smacked with the back of Kyvain's hand in a manly gesture that, in previous generations, would have been a summon to stand as second in a duel.

Two against one aren't bad odds, but Aric's clearly the kind of man who defies mathematics. Attacking Aric would be suicide, but I won't say a word if this is how Kyvain decides to die.

Unfortunately, I'm out of time to witness his demise. Moonlight kisses the tops of the trees and the buzz under my skin has grown from a mere itch into a searing need to shift.

I have more questions than I can count, but it seems they're going to have to wait.

Pain splinters through me.

The deafening howl of my wolf splits my skull with its intensity. Bending at the waist, I dig my fingers into my hair with a silent scream.

The Dark Moon has officially begun.

Chapter Five

Dark Moon

Rhys

Magic lashes out like a wave of chaos.

Kyvain and Calvin both pant heavily as the moonlight washes over them, calling to the wolves buried inside their souls. Twin agonizing cries break past their lips, and Kyvain sends one last angry glare toward Aric.

"This isn't over," he threatens, but his voice is rough, not nearly as human as it was a few minutes prior.

"Anytime, *boy*." Aric grins with pure manic amusement. It's scary as fuck. "In this realm or the next." Pressing on his knuckles, he cracks them like this is some bad eighties mafia movie, but somehow the gesture looks completely natural on him. Like he's used to threatening people daily.

Maybe he fucking is.

Why doesn't that make me want to run? The warmth in my chest pushes me to get closer, but the pain tearing at my joints makes me stumble toward the woods while I still remain upright.

Cold sweat breaks out across my brow. A whimper cries from my lips.

Three monstrous steps is all it takes for Aric to reach my side.

He doesn't hook a finger under my chin all gentle and sweet. He full out grabs my chin, his fingers pressing into my cheeks as he lifts my entire face up to stare into his soulless gaze.

This close, I can see the scar that lines one eye, slashing straight through his brow and leaving a pink, jagged line I want to trace with the tip of my finger. And his eyes. They're so much more vibrant this close. Hellfire spits at the center of the golden brown irises. I have no doubt this man doesn't belong here.

They're like burning comets streaking across a pitch-black sky. Flecks of gold glitter in the dark depths, warming them.

I'm fucking transfixed, even as my body tries to turn itself inside out.

"What's wrong?" he booms, the demand thick and consuming. I couldn't deny answering him if I wanted to. And I don't.

My wolf yearns to draw closer.

"First shift…" It's all I can get out of my raw

throat. Swallowing jagged glass would be less painful, but I've survived a hell of a lot in my twenty-one years, and I'm not about to let this shift break me. If I can get through this, everything will get easier. If the old wolves are to be believed, every subsequent shift after the first hurts less and less until it's as easy and natural as breathing.

A flash of fire consumes the frost kissed air, warming it until I shiver from the change in temperature against my skin.

God, he's such a drama queen with these combustible entrances. Is it really necessary right now?

Starlit blue eyes search mine as the burning man from earlier today studies my face, looking for a lie that's not there.

"You've never shifted before?" More shock and confusion. I've never been this awe-inspiring before. Mysterious and confusing aren't two words anyone in this pack would associate with me—unless they were talking about the animal ready to rip its way out of my chest.

"Why does everything I say confuse you? I'm not the one who keeps reappearing in a burst of fucking fire here." It doesn't come out as snarky as I wanted, the pain is stealing my breath at this point.

"We can't take her," the burning man whispers.

"We—"

A groan of agony ripping up my throat cuts Aric off, and both of them side-eye me like my pain is really getting in the way of a very important meeting right now.

"We're taking her, Latham." Aric turns fully to me and just as I stumble, my backbone twisting and shifting abnormally, he catches me. "There's no fucking way I'm leaving her with this shitty pack."

He saves me once more.

Only to toss my ass over his shoulder like yesterday's trash, ready for the dump.

"Let's go, Love."

"I-I'm going to do something bad," I confess as rage and snapping snarls fall from my lips.

"Don't we all?" is all he says.

"She's not ours to take," Latham argues, but it's a rather careless statement. There's no fight in his words. Just total calm in his warm tone.

It almost makes me forget about the agony clawing into my back with each passing second.

My head bounces off of the hardness of Aric's spine, and I barely realize we've stopped.

"Back for more already?" Aric's low tone is sarcastic in a deadly way, but it's only when I catch the same familiar musk I've grown up hating that I comprehend who must be standing ahead of us. This whole not being able to see thing has it disadvantages, but as I stare at Aric's ass, I know I've got the better view.

My captor shifts me on his shoulder like he can easily kill Kyvain with one hand and hold me hostage with the other. I don't doubt his multitasking skills, but right now, I can barely focus through the violent

magic tearing through my body to decide which man is the lesser of two evils.

"Where the fuck are you taking her?" Kyvain growls savagely.

"Home." The word falls from Aric's lips like he won't entertain any further conversation on the subject. It's not up for debate. It's a fact, but I also think it's a lie.

"She can see herself home. My father, the alpha, wasn't aware we were receiving visitors this evening. If you want to keep breathing, I suggest you pay him the respect he deserves, state your intentions, and submit." Kyvain smiles cruelly, like he's bested Aric somehow.

"We're just passing through," Latham states while Aric simply snarls. I have a feeling rules mean nothing to either of them. I envy that freedom.

"Then be on your way," Kyvain orders darkly. "And leave my *property* behind."

"I'll never be your property," I snap harshly.

"Try again, Rhys. The deal is done. By daybreak, you'll be mine, so you better go home and get some rest." His promise sends another shuddering chill down my spine. "But before you go, I just wanted to tell you one more thing," I hear Kyvain say in a voice far too animalistic and smug for someone shifting into a beast the way I am.

Gods, did he take a fucking magical Tylenol before this shit?

"Fuck off!" Aric growls, his hold tightening

around me.

"I wanted her to know whose mating mark claimed me tonight."

My jaw splinters with pain as the bones beneath my skin shifts and sharp teeth fill my mouth, but I'm listening past the agony. My fists dig into Aric's shirt, letting him know I want to hear what the asshole has to say. Because he wouldn't come back to taunt me unless he had a bomb ready to destroy my life.

"Your sweet little friend Bea claimed my mating mark." His words chill me, freezing my heart in a block of ice so thick it might never recover. "Her wolf found me. Ran right up to me like the good little bitch she is."

I angle myself as much as I can, only to find a beautiful raven-haired wolf sitting at Kyvain's feet. Her head is lowered down, but bright blue eyes peer up at me. It's her. The same floral scent she's always had tickles my nose, even as the bones there break and start to reform. My lungs squeeze in on themselves until they're no longer functional and all I can think about is how she crushed on the shyest boy in our village for the last two years.

Only to claim Kyvain as her mate.

"The moon hasn't finished claiming me yet, but my time is coming soon. I can feel it. Any minute now, the mating will be complete," Kyvain says proudly as his already sharpened fingers dig into Bea's beautiful fur at the back of her wolf's neck.

No! No, no, no!

"And I'll be finding you soon too," he whispers

with a cruel smile cutting across his lips.

Aric steps forward hard, his chest knocking into Kyvain's.

He's ready and waiting for violence all the time it seems.

But so is my wolf.

Magic strikes through me with the force of lightning, leaving hot embers burning through my veins. Warmth sears every inch of me. A rush of power and pain collide in a distortion of cracking bones that overtakes my body.

In a gracefully swift movement only my wolf could make, I leap off of Aric's back and attack. My nails dig into skin as I launch myself forward hard. My jaws open as a growl straight from hell tears up my throat. Hot blood fills my mouth as my teeth sink into weak flesh, the scent of Kyvain seeming so much stronger as he bleeds. A scream of agony is a whisper of sound in my ears as my pulse pounds louder and louder, but it gets lost in the sea of cries from all the wolves shifting for the first time tonight.

The pack doesn't know their precious golden son needs help. The shadows of night cloak us, and this chance at revenge is a gift I can't refuse.

Powerful jaws wrench sideways as my wolf shakes her head, her whole body following through with the violent movement, and meat tears from the limb in a satisfying slick sound.

Kyvain cries out once more before he stumbles away, leaning on a stunned Calvin for support while a familiar dark wolf whimpers at his feet. They don't cry out to bring the enforcers down on my head. They just stare, shocked.

Blood soaks through my enemy's shirt, darkening around his upper arm where his flesh that still fills my snout is a divot of muscle within his shoulder.

Russet eyes lock on my blue ones. Aric must see the pain and rage reflected inside my gaze, because his becomes downright murderous when he looks to Kyvain again.

But the moon will claim us all tonight.

Kyvain drops to his knees with more screams that bleed into the cries of others going through the same torture. Calvin stumbles back from his friend, his own shift on the brink, and Bea lies down, her eyes sad and forlorn. Cracking and cries snap through the night as his wolf breaks his feeble body.

It happens much faster for him.

The golden alpha boy doesn't suffer nearly enough.

I linger and watch as his clothes shed to the snowy ground in tattered strips and flesh rips away from a timber colored wolf possibly three times my size.

My white fur reflects in the depths of his cold blue eyes as his beast looks upon me for the first time.

And something unimaginably terrible happens.

Kyvain's howl rips through the night in a way only an alpha's could. It draws a crowd, the other pack members and wolves on the hill heeding his call.

His wolf brings one large paw forward, he comes ever so close to me… and then lowers his head as far down to the ground as he can manage.

"The mating pose," a woman hisses like a curse.

What. The. fuck.

"Kyvain's wolf, the alpha's son, chose the outcast," someone else whispers.

No.

No. No. No. No.

The big innocent eyes of the raven-haired wolf look up at me. Bea looks at me with a new kind of pain and hurt.

Her mate… chose me.

I shake my head hard.

A whimper crawls over my lips, but I can't say a word to my friend. My best friend. My *only* friend.

I step away from Kyvain. One foot after the other, I move through the crowd that hisses and whispers. Aric and Latham are nowhere to be found now that there are too many people surrounding us, but I feel them nearby all the same like guardian angels.

The crowd parts like I'm a leper, and they let me go.

Until Kyvain's wolf becomes a bigger asshole than himself.

The wolf strides toward me. I know what he wants.

He said it himself. He wanted to make me his whore. I just don't think he anticipated his wolf making me its mate. But I know he'll take what he wants regardless.

My wolf snarls. Magic blooms through me, and then I'm running. My feet move at a pounding rhythm that seems faster than the beating of my heart. My wolf wants to turn around and rip him to shreds, but I just can't allow her to do that.

I can't kill him.

A growl of disagreement snarls up my throat. She's furious I'm running away, saving her from the tortuous death our pack would give us if I let her kill him.

Every prickle of sound stings my ears. I hear their war cries. The alpha calls out for someone to capture the woman who harmed his son.

He clearly doesn't know his son is hell-bent on doing that himself. A barking command sounds somewhere just behind me, but I don't pause for a single second to look back at my tormentor. The pavement is slick as the grassy land disappears, and I come to the intersection of the town square.

A white light shines up ahead, and the doors to the school are haloed just beneath the bright lamp.

Shit.

I look to the right and left, but cottages surround us. Homes and families and maybe even small children may be inside by now.

I can't bring a dog fight into someone's fucking living room.

Once more, my wolf grunts in disagreement.

I mentally roll my eyes at her fuck-all nature.

My paws pound over the icy road and up the small

front steps, and I take the deepest breath just before the enormous white wolf of mine launches herself through a solid sheet of glass. The door shatters around me, debris raining down across my fur.

But I keep on going.

A clatter of sound tells me Kyvain is hot on my tail, and there's the smallest part of me that's ready to let my beast turn and confront him just like she wants to.

I just… I can't kill him. I can't kill someone. I can't do it.

Dark tile floors shine in the densely dark hall. I hear his nails clicking closer and closer. Sharp claws sink into my back. Magic roars to life inside me, and it sparks so violently it blows out in waves. A shattering of glass crackles to the floor on all sides. Papers and pens fall around me. Assignments drift through the shadowy hallway.

Because my wolf stops dead in her tracks to look upon the man who dares dishonor her.

Easy girl, I coo thoughtlessly.

She doesn't even acknowledge me as her sharp teeth snap at the cowering wolf who stands in the middle of the chaotic mess I've made.

If he attacks, if he tries anything stupid—and let's face it, it's just a matter of time for this asshole—my wolf will rip his throat out without a second glance.

And I'll be forever a lone wolf, rejected from her pack.

Or dead.

Kyvain's head is lowered, but he stalks carefully around me. I sense him, and I sense his curious stupidity too.

Easy, I say once more at the back of our mind.

But she shakes her head slowly with a rising growl that hums across the gray metal lockers.

Kyvain lowers in a pounce that says our time is running out. I lower my own stance as well. I'll kill him. I'll kill him for every single thing he's ever done or would have done to Bea and myself.

Time slows as I assess every move he makes.

His body tenses to a crouch, his teeth bared. Then he leaps.

A flash of fire burns through the darkness. It sparks across my fur as strong arms wrap around me from out of nowhere. A new calming scent washes over me, and even the recklessness of my beast relaxes against his chest.

"Let's get you out of here, Love," the burning man whispers like a promise.

And in a hot flash of hellacious flames, the world burns away into dust.

Or so it feels.

Chapter Six

A Fairytale

Aric

He cradles her naked body against him as if he actually fucking gives a shit about this one.

I've been running realm tasks for Hela for thousands of years. Not once has Latham ever gone out of his way for anyone.

"Why's she naked?" Torben grunts.

"Because shifters can't summon a wardrobe with the snap of a finger, dumbass," Latham answers, but he doesn't give a fuck enough to glance his way.

Torben thinks he's the leader every time we step foot out of Hell. It's the half giant in him. They think everything they stomp on is theirs.

I'll let him think whatever he wants. No scales off my tail. But Latham, I think he was born to hate the gods.

And Torben, he might live in Hell, but he's every bit a warrior of the heavens.

"The bigger question is why is she a shifter at all?" I whisper as I look down on the beautiful blonde-haired vixen.

Her lashes never flutter, but something feels off...

"Who are you guys?" she asks as she casually opens her eyes to the three men staring down on her.

She looks to each of us without an ounce of terror or fear brightening her gaze.

She's either fearless or has known fear too often within her life.

"We're hell sent," Latham answers freely.

Her brow scrunches, and this shit is not going the way I imagined. I thought we'd have to drag this girl to Hell. She's lounging in Latham's arms right now like he's a fucking man-hammock.

"Is that a pack? Where is it located?"

My lips twitch with a smile.

"In Hell," I answer all too gruffly.

Latham shoots me a look, but I won't sugar coat it. What's the point? And yeah... maybe I want her to put up a little fight. See if she's as powerful as Hela makes her out to be.

She blinks slowly at that, and I see her chewing it around in her pretty little head.

Still isn't running or screaming though…

Hmm.

"You know, the place of eternal suffering and such," I add, and I swear Latham's death glare just shot beams my way.

Why's she so calm? Where is the screaming and running?

I listen intently, and her pulse is soaring faster than when she was in her wolf form.

So she is afraid.

She's just very, very good at hiding it.

It's then that she slips out of Latham's arms and I note the way he drags her down his body before letting her feet touch the leafy ground. I arch a brow at him, but he just shakes his head at my suggestive smirk. He hovers near her, obviously prepared to catch her should she fall, faint, or just keel the fuck over.

Must be fucking exhausting being that nice.

Latham sparks a flame in his hand. It sizzles hotly against the chill in the air before black clothing and a pair of boots appear there.

He hands them to her, and she takes a step back, turning away as she changes quickly right in front of us. My gaze slides down the nice arch of her back toward the curve of her ass, and I have to look away as a rumble of sound I can't control crawls up my throat.

I shove my hands deep in my pockets as I wait, but I'm clearly not cut out for this gentleman shit. Latham always makes it seem so easy. It's fucking not.

Because I look again. White frost kisses her pale hair in the shine of the moonlight as the snow continues to fall lightly around us. She's beautiful in that pure, don't-fuck-up-the-innocent kind of way.

Tonight played out like a fucking fairy tale. We saved the girl. Funny how story books make dragons and monsters like us out to be the ones you rescue the girl from, not the other way around.

She pulls her last boot on and turns to assess us more carefully.

"What do you guys want with me?" she finally asks. I realize how much farther she's stepped away from us while she changed. Two yards now lie safely between her and us.

We're just on the outskirts of her pack's territory, between their land and the Ice Mountains. She could make it back to those tormenting assholes in about five   minutes   if   she   shifted. "You don't belong here," Torben says in a deep, rumbling tone. She peers up at the half giant. He's intimidating. Nearly seven feet tall of solid, impatient strength.

Only person that has the balls to test the demigod is Latham. Which is odd to me since I've never seen the shapeshifter throw a punch in his entire life.

"I know that. Thanks." Her bright blue eyes narrow on Torben, and I'm not going to say it, but maybe we should leave the small talk to Latham. He's good at that shit, making women feel all warm and fuzzy and shit.

Let him do the hard part.

"You don't fit in with your pack because you belong in Hell," Latham explains, his honey accent is all calm waves of relaxation and circle jerks.

Yeah. Girls like that shit.

She closes her eyes and a long, tired sigh slips from her lips.

Hmm. She's not loving it the way women usually do when Latham talks.

"Try again," I whisper to my friend.

He glances my way with a mixture of bewilderment and annoyance crinkling the corner of his eyes.

I wave a hand between him and her like it's obvious, but now they're both sighing at me.

Whatever that passive hostility means.

"You mentioned my mother," she whispers, and the deepest, saddest blue eyes look to Latham like she could drown him in the depths of her oceanic gaze.

He nods.

She lowers her head, and I can see her thinking this through. Her pack doesn't want her. Hell, after tonight, I wouldn't be surprised if they're ordered to kill her, much less shun her. The little fucker who threatened her flashes before my eyes, and I make a mental note to run one last *errand* before we head for the Ice Mountains.

She has nothing here. And we can take her to her mother. Her homeland.

Her place in life…

We've more than proved that we have the magic

to make those things happen for her.

She's really taking her sweet-ass time thinking this over though.

My fingers drum against my thigh as I wait.

And wait.

Fuck. Who has this kind of patience?

Rhys eyes her pack's territory, and then us, and then back again like she's truly weighing her limited options. Finally, a defeated sigh breaks past her lips.

"Okay," she says with a slow nod that I think is meant to reassure herself rather than us.

"Okay!" I clap my hands with a wide smile that just seems to set her even more on edge. "Okay," I try again with less enthusiasm and a smaller smile of encouragement.

She still looks at me like she isn't sure if I'll help her or kill her.

"Okay," I say one more time so quietly the effort drifts off into total nothingness, and at this point, I need to just let it the fuck go.

"I want to go home first."

Torben shakes his head. "Can't go back to the village. We have to keep moving."

"I'm leaving my adoptive mom, my best friend, and my entire life behind on a half-ass chance that you guys can actually take me to my mother. I'm not leaving my cat to die in my bedroom because Mary can't be bothered to feed the poor thing. It's just not right."

"Your adoptive mom's a cunt, your best friend

mated with your prick of an enemy, and your cat will be fucking fine," I tell her, but the flinch of her gaze and the hard pull of her brow tells me those words may have sounded a bit harsher out loud than I intended.

"He'll be fine," I try once more in a softer yet still growling tone.

Her glare is still a look of hellfire. It's a death threat she gives to me, Torben, and even Latham.

So... I guess we'll be making a pit stop for a fucking house cat.

Chapter Seven

Wolf in Sheep's Clothing

Rhys

The tall man stays in the woods as Aric wraps me up in his arms without provocation.

Between one breath and the next, shadows crawl over Aric's tattooed skin, extending to creep over onto my own. A feeling as deep and dark as despair seeps into me. It spreads through my chest with a ferocity that makes me cling with bruising force to the asshole who pulled me against him without so much as a warning.

My anger sits heavily on my tongue, but I can barely squeak past Latham's heavy stare. His gaze traces the way Aric's arms band around my body before he goes up in another poof of fire,

in a way I'm growing used to.

What the hell am I doing with these three?

"Buckle up, buttercup." Aric's dark tone sucks all the humor out of his words. He should really stick to being scary, humor isn't a good look on him. Or perhaps he's more terrifying when he's trying to lighten the mood.

I don't get another second to contemplate as the same dizzying, shadowy void descends. It presses in on me with a pressure that might kill me if I take a single breath. It eats us up. Then it spits us back out in some other place.

Aric releases me long before I'm ready, and I nearly fall to the chilled ground as my lungs heave. The air around me fills with that smoky steam you get when you exhale warm breath into winter air.

Latham's hand strokes soothingly over my back until I'm ready, and then he guides me through the shroud of woods covering us. It takes a minute for my brain to catch up with the speed things are coming at me, but I realize we're still blocks away from my cottage.

"It was safer not to take you directly to your front door in case they're waiting for you," Latham explains, and I nod, like this is all completely normal.

Not one thing about this day has been fucking normal though.

I know if my pack catches me, I'm as good as dead. And if by some miracle they let me survive, my fate as the pack whore is sealed.

I'm out of options, except to play out the offer from these hellish men.

Aric and Latham jump a tall wooden fence and I follow. We land on our feet, me with a bit more of a stumble than the two infernal men at my side. They peer around at the village, the park benches abandoned with only a layer of snow now decorating them in the quiet of the night.

"The snow's getting heavier," Latham whispers as we keep to the shadows, heading toward the row of cottages and tromping through their backyards.

"It shouldn't be snowing," I comment offhandedly, peering up at the flurries that are only growing thicker.

"End of Days," Aric grumbles oddly, and my brows pull down as I stare up at the towering beast of a man next to me.

I collect their words, but really, I'm just buying time while we head back to the home I grew up in. I don't know where I'll end up at the end of this messy night, but I know I can't trust them. It balances out to about as much as I can trust my own pack though, and that's sad.

Asking for my cat was more of a test. If I'm a hostage to them, they would take me with or without my approval. But I'm not a hostage it seems, and they're not violent.

Toward me anyway…

Do I believe them enough to find out if they can take me to my mother, someone who has been a mystery to me my entire life?

I guess we'll see.

"No, it's because of us. We've been in one place too long. We're affecting their world." Latham scans the night with a casual sweep of his gaze.

"You're claiming responsibility for the snow?" It's half a scoff, but then reality sets in. I've legit seen these guys disappear into thin air. Fuck, they just transported me in the same shroud of darkness. Deep down, part of me registers what they say as truth. I even thought as much myself.

They're not from here. And if they're not from here...

"Hell creatures shouldn't be in the Realm of the Living. It throws everything off balance." Latham catches my hand, and I stiffen hard before he points down in front of me and I realize I'm half an inch away from falling face first over a tricycle in the dark.

"Thanks," I whisper and he slides his hand down my wrist as he releases me swiftly. His words linger in my mind as much as his smooth touch lingers on my skin. It's not hard to imagine these men as some kind of demons. I've grown up hearing the stories of the light and dark gods. Once upon a time, shifters used to think our magic was a gift from the gods themselves, but over time that belief faded until it became nothing more than fairy-tale fodder. Now, I'm questioning everything.

If wolf shifters exist—a hard and true fact in my life—what else does?

Somehow the words are forced from my mouth, my curiosity eating away at me. "Am I a Hell creature?"

"In a way." Latham shrugs like he's not changing my whole life with three small words. "All magic comes from one of the nine realms. Some, like Torben, are a mixture of magic. Just like you." Latham kicks a soccer ball out of my way just before my foot nearly rolls off of it.

He keeps his watchful eyes searching the perimeter, but he seems unnaturally aware of everything and everyone.

"Nine realms?" I ask as we turn down my street.

"Fucking grocery list of locations: Asgard, Midgard, which is the Realm of the Living, places with giants, places with elves, places with dwarves, places with just fucking beasts on fire," Aric rumbles off some examples.

"The emptiness where you come from," Latham scoffs with a sexy smirk that reveals a dimple just above the corner of his lip.

"Fuck you! Don't mock my home. I will strip your flesh down to bones and feast on the sloppy leftovers." Aric shoves his hands into his pockets as he mumbles something about dragon magic.

"You're a dragon shifter?" I look at the tattooed man at my side, trying to figure him out.

He peers at me with that magic burning in a ring around his pupils, then he nods. My attention slides down his muscular frame, the hard build of his posture and even the rough caress of every word he speaks. He truly seems like a dragon in a man's body. He appears more beast than he is man.

"And you're…" I glance at Latham.

"A fenrir. Son of Loki. My inner shifter is a hellhound. I try not to let him out too often."

Something about the way he phrases it makes me prod further. "But you can shapeshift into other things… people even?"

He nods. "The magic of the gods," he tells me.

The oddity of Mrs. Linskey's behavior tonight circles my mind. She's most likely curled up in her favorite afghan at home watching reruns of *The Price Is Right*. She was never in that clearing, and that chills me to the bone more than the snow ever could.

Latham is a wolf in sheep's clothing.

He might be the most dangerous one of all.

"And the other man, Torben. Can he shift?" The desire to know them and figure out what I'm up against keeps the questions flowing off my tongue.

Latham smirks.

"No," he replies.

"Well. That's not entirely true," Aric says with a sharp smile slicing up his lips. "He quite frequently shifts into a total jackass."

Latham closes his eyes hard as a wide smile overtakes his handsome face. But then he stops in his tracks, then nods to the small cottage with the blue shutters.

"That's your place," Latham whispers.

My chin lifts and just seeing my house grounds me. The loneliness and the hurt of the last fourteen years slams into me all at once.

Why am I coming back to all of that?
And if I could, would I truly want to stay?

Chapter Eight

Here, Kitty Kitty

Latham

The lights are off in the small cottage. I don't sense a soul, but I hold Rhys back, keeping her hidden in the shadows. Just to make sure.

We didn't come all this way to fuck up over a house cat.

Not that apprehending the girl Hela sent us to collect has gone all that smoothly.

Never once have I run into a person quite like Rhys.

Usually mere mortals cower from the sight of us. Or piss themselves after witnessing our infernal powers.

It's like their puny little brains can't handle the truth of the world and their insignificant place in it.

But this girl? She's a fucking anomaly.

Or maybe she just has no common sense for fear.

A more likely possibility.

Still, the small voice in the back of my mind is reminding me that despite the way Rhys has grown up, she's no mere mortal, or even a regular shifter for that matter. She just doesn't realize it yet.

Rhys is silent at my side, eyes trained on the dark windows of the cottage. Her light blonde hair is nearly as pale as the moonlight, and the deepening night makes her ocean blue eyes appear more like sapphires. And her face... it's far too delicate. A blush covers the perfect arches of her cheekbones which frame the pink bow of her lips. Compared to Aric, Torben, and myself, she's tiny. The top of her head falls at Aric's shoulder. I'm only slightly shorter than the dragon, and standing this close to Rhys, I have to peer down to take her in.

Nothing about this girl deserves what we're going to do to her.

The weight of the invisible shackles on my wrists burn with the heat of my sworn allegiance.

Rhys gazes up at me. Her attention is like hellfire across my skin, making me all too aware of her captivating eyes. It's her strange magic... I think. I quickly turn away while grinding my teeth. My jaw jumps as I nod toward the house.

"I think it's safe to go inside," I say, ready to get

her cat and get the fuck out of here. Besides the fact that I don't like the danger we're putting Rhys in, if we don't get going soon, we'll be facing a much greater danger.

The one where I change my mind and report back to my sister that we never found the girl. Because this girl—she's too innocent for the Realm of Hell.

I can tell she doesn't belong, and I've barely known her for a few hours.

Aric looks over at me with a hard glare that says he knows what I'm thinking. Unlike me, he's not ready to risk my sister's wrath. Without hesitation, his hand wraps around Rhys's bicep and he tugs her roughly forward. She has to stumble to keep up with his long strides, and I smirk to see the little thing seethe.

"You don't have to manhandle me to go inside. I'm pretty sure I was the one who demanded we come back for my cat." Without a care for the bruise that will be left on her flesh, she wrenches herself out of his grip with more strength than I gave her petite little frame credit for.

I can't help the smirk that lifts my lips.

Striding forward with the confidence of a goddess, she bends, giving us a perfect view of her pretty little ass. I'm still staring at the rounded curves when Aric marches forward with the intent of kicking in the door.

"No!" Rhys screeches, straightens, and rushes Aric with another tiny sword in her hand that she procured from a plastic rock sitting on the front stoop.

Humans are weird. Get bigger swords and better

hiding places, for the love of the gods.

Sick amusement crosses Aric's face as he stares down at the brandished 'key' Rhys told me about earlier.

Not like any key I remember.

"It's going to take a lot more than this toothpick to kill me, kitten." Aric flicks the metal with his index finger.

"For fuck's sake!" Rhys grumbles and shoves the man out of her way. "I'm not trying to kill you, I'm trying to unlock the fucking door. What is it with you guys and modern-day locking systems?"

Stabbing the tiny sword into the handle of the door, like wounding it will make it open before us, Rhys shoves her shoulder into the door and it does in fact creak open on hinges that could use some oil.

"Kicking it would have been faster," Aric muses, rubbing at the shadow of scruff on his jaw.

"And more destructive," Rhys scolds like that makes any fucking difference to us.

"Oftentimes, destruction is better," my friend murmurs.

She ignores him entirely as she enters. We step inside, and Rhys immediately heads down the hallway for her room.

"This is where you live?" Aric glares around menacingly, and I wonder if he's having the same thoughts I did.

This shithole is no place for Rhys.

She deserves better. More.

Not that any of us are planning to do any better by her.

Fucking hell.

Literally.

"Yeah. This is home sweet home," Rhys calls from the vicinity of her room.

I stride down the dark hallway and lean against the doorframe while Aric mumbles about being able to cross the whole damn house in six fucking steps.

I'm pretty sure he's testing his theory, if the loud clomping is any indication.

The real problem is… there isn't one picture of the girl who lives in this house. There's a fine portrait of a rather pretentious-looking woman hanging near the door, but there are no prideful displays of the beautiful and strong woman before me.

"I was right! Fucking six." Aric grumbles.

I don't turn to tell him six of his dragon steps equals about twelve human steps. Rhys scurries around her small room, glancing toward the window more than once as if she's worried the boogeyman is going to leap out and grab her.

Too bad something way more fucked up has already descended into her life. And the two fucked up bastards are now helping her look for a gods damned cat.

When did I get demoted like this?

Ripping open the drawers of her dresser, she shoves some articles of clothing into an emptied out bookbag. Shirts, shorts, jeans, and socks. Lastly, she grabs a handful of undergarments. Hot pink lace spills out of the side of her bag, and I can't stay still any longer.

I wander over, one silent step at a time, kneeling before her until the tiny scrap of fabric dangles off my fingertips.

"This is what you pack when you're on the run?"

Rhys's gaze starts at my chest and slowly caresses my body until she's staring into my eyes, each of our blue gazes in a battle of wills. Her gaze is like a touch of hot, powerful magic tingling across my flesh.

Warmth works into her cheeks, nearly the same color of the sexy thong. "It's rude to paw at a woman's underwear." She snatches the lace from my finger and shoves it down deep into the little bag.

The hiss of a cat punctuates her words, as do the thudding footsteps of Aric. The asshole isn't even trying to be quiet with his approach.

"Packing the essentials, I see." He grins, the smile more feral than a stray cat.

"Almost done," Rhys tells us before slipping her cellphone into the front pocket of her bag.

"Like fuck." Aric's growl bounces off the white walls of the bedroom. Moving into the room, he reaches for the bag and hauls the phone out of it before breaking it in half as if it were a measly twig instead of the metal and glass that rains to the floor in little clatters.

"What the hell, asshole?" Rhys snaps, pushing against Aric's chest like she's a god that can move mountains.

I roll my eyes as I watch the shitshow, but Aric's molten gaze is already spitting hellfire. He loves the challenge.

"Who do you have in this life that you'd call anyway?" he taunts. He's not wrong.

All he has to do is walk forward, and Rhys stumbles back.

"You're not going to need a communication device where you're going," he promises.

"Bad reception," I joke, attempting to dilute the thick tension in the air, but it falls on deaf ears as an angry mewling hisses through the room.

The small gray cat Rhys named after my father slinks out from under the bed to weave between her legs, his tail wrapping around one shin. It stands before her like a guardian, and I find a new respect for the tiny creature. It's loyal, which is one of its only redeeming attributes. Why humans are determined to keep pets, I'll never understand.

"What do we have here?" Aric stoops and hauls the cat up by its scruff, letting it dangle in front of his face as he studies the feline with drawn brows. "Looks like a snack."

"Give me back my cat, or there's no way in hell I'm going with you. You almost had me fooled, but you're nothing more than a fucking psycho!" Rhys accuses with a hard glare in her eyes, but I see the sliver of fear for Loki in her steadfast gaze. It would take Aric no time to crush the thing. If he shifted, he's right, the cat would be no more than a tasty morsel for his dragon.

Fuck knows he's eaten far less savory meals in the pits of Hell.

"You don't have much of a choice, kitten. Stay here and you die."

"There's always the suburbs." A shiver works through Rhys, and I swear she thinks that's the more hellish option than coming with us. If only she knew. Suburban housewives have nothing on me.

"Aric!" I scold, needing to shut this shit down and act as the buffer between the two once more. Every minute we spend here is a risk I'm done taking, but that's all I have time to get out.

Magic tingles in the air and then zaps through it like lightning. Aric's growl of pain is almost as surprising as the rip of fur and the harsh mewl that crawls down my spine like nails on a chalkboard. Not even Hell's creatures are immune to that fucking sound.

In fact, it's one of our more creative punishments for the wicked.

An afterlife of that sound grating on your ears is enough to drive anyone utterly insane. I know, because I've withstood that punishment.

Several times.

Where there was once a small gray cat now stands a monstrous feline as large as a lion and twice as fierce. Of course she would have a guardian. I almost kick myself for not realizing it sooner, except watching it attack my friend is worth the entertainment. Razor-

sharp teeth sink into Aric's meaty thigh, and he curses with the force of the strongest tempest as he tries to dislodge its jagged maw.

"This thing better have its fucking rabies shot," he grits out as it slashes at his arms with razor-sharp claws.

"Loki?" Rhys squeaks in a terror-ridden pitch, her hands white knuckling her bag as she backs up until she hits the wall. Not Kyvain, not the information about taking her to Hell, not even the news I dropped about her mom made her eyes this wide. But watching her tiny cat turn into a guardian from Hell seems to have broken her brain.

"Fucking hellcats!" Aric spews as he fights off the predator determined to slash him to ribbons.

I chuckle. "Here, kitty kitty." The coo is a melody filled with sarcasm as I watch Aric struggle—until the beast's slitted eyes lock on me. Then it lunges.

"Fuck!" Flames shoot from my hands in a whirl of magic until I'm holding a fireblade. My arms lift with an arc of power. I lash out, and then swallow when the blade does nothing but swish through the cat's fiery image without injury. The fire of my weapon is consumed, leaving me defenseless from the snapping jaws. The bones of the hellcat are cast in a shadowy glow as flames illuminate its insides.

I barely have time to whisk away in smoky magic before it shoots fire back at my face, trying to singe off my goddamn eyebrows.

Together, Aric and I work to tame the fucker, or at least that's what I'm trying to do. I have a feeling

Rhys will never forgive us if we kill her beloved cat—hellish guardian or not. I flicker in several times here and there, taunting it away from my friend, but it's clear Aric doesn't give a single fuck if the cat lives. With every vicious attack, he's clearly trying to end its immortal life.

Claw marks tatter the wall in thick lines. The scent of fire is heavy in the air. Drops of blood are flung all over the floor with every lashing move Aric makes.

"Loki," Rhys says in a steady tone, a whisper so quiet I barely hear it.

Big beastly eyes finally look away from us. Then, without warning, the hellcat shifts again, falling to tiny feet that pad happily out of the room and bound out of the open door.

My arms sting from the razor-thin cuts it slashed into my skin, and Aric's leg is bleeding profusely. Dark blood coats the floor of Rhys's bedroom, turning it into a more murderous scene than before.

I look up to find her. I expect her to be huddled in the corner, away from the mess we've created of her room. My stomach drops instantly. Slowly, my eyes harden to ice as they clash with the angry fire in Aric's.

"She's fucking gone!"

Chapter Nine

Four Mates

Rhys

In a matter of minutes, I'm nearing the fence with a small—possibly deadly—cat in my bag. I run so fast I can't even feel the ground beneath my feet. It's exhilarating to see how much faster and stronger I am since letting my wolf out into the world.

Loki lets out a low disgruntled meow whenever the bag jostles against my back.

"It's okay, pretty boy," I coo, but I have no idea if I'm saying the right thing.

My house cat almost killed a dragon shifter.

And that fucking dragon shifter almost killed my innocent pet.

Would those men kill me too if I became too much of a hassle for them? They led me on with talk of my mother, but they insulted me when they continuously threw it in my face that I have no one and nothing here.

I do have a friend. A bond with someone that's stronger than family.

Bea's like a sister to me.

I just hope she still feels that way after everything that happened tonight. I'll lay low for a while and then try to come back, explain and apologize for attacking her mate… my mate…

Shit. Everything's a mess.

I shake it all away and just focus on getting the hell away from this pack and my new hellish friends.

At that thought, feet pound over the dirt behind me, and though I'm fast, they match my speed.

Dirt flings in the air as I turn on my boots and face the assholes.

Except… it's a different asshole.

Kyvain.

And he's brought friends.

Bea stands wide-eyed behind him, and she's all I can focus on right now.

"Bea," I whisper.

She lifts her big green eyes up to me, but a new mark glows white against her neck. Her mating mark. She flinches as it burns brighter before she lowers her gaze and stares at the ground.

"What the fuck did you do to her?" I accuse, looking Kyvain's arrogant ass in the eyes.

His arm is bandaged tightly, but a dark red stain spreads from his shoulder downward.

Good.

"You planning on leaving? Never coming back?" Kyvain's lips twist into a cruel smirk, and before I can say anything, he cuts me off. "My mate isn't going anywhere just yet."

"I'm not your mate." My chin lifts, and I'm absolutely right.

Bea wears his mark, a slashing of three lines along her neck. I note a faint white scar branding the back of his hand with a new mark, a moon on fire it seems.

"My mark looks pretty on you. I like the way you wear it," I whisper to him sweetly, a real fuck you. I want him to understand that he doesn't own me.

If anything, I own him now.

Calvin and two other men in the shadows shift on their feet.

"We uh… we were all marked, Rhys," Calvin says to me as if it might be an error of the Dark Moon that I might be able to fix.

"All four of you are marked as mine?" I ask with narrowed eyes, and really, this is getting entirely too fucked up.

They all nod.

Maybe it's karma. This is what you get when you torment someone all your life.

Now you're forced to love her for all eternity.

And she'll never love you back.

Never.

I shake my head slowly and pause on Bea once more.

"I love you, Bea. I'll find you again someday," I whisper, knowing now I have to leave for longer than I ever anticipated, and just before I turn toward the fence, her bright eyes smile back at me with a hint of sadness and love shining within.

My fingers dig into cold, snow slicked timber, but just as I lift my leg against it, a hand wraps around my ankle and jerks me back down. I stagger down and strong hands pin me to the fence. Wood bites into my spine while my hands are pulled up high, and Kyvain's raging blue eyes glare down on me.

"You fucking bit me, you whore!"

My knee comes up hard and fast, and he crumbles to the ground even faster. The three men who surrounded him earlier lunge forward. I never flinch, but the violence I anticipate never comes.

They leap onto my lifelong tormentor, and angry kicks and punches are thrown at him.

"Don't fucking touch her!" they roar with newfound loyalty.

"Ever."

But an alpha has more power than three confused mates.

Kyvain thrashes out with a roar of power and all three of them cower back.

One of them peers up, his blond head still down

turned but his eyes searing into mine with aggression and confusion as he says, "Alpha Morganson said you're not coming back. You're not welcome anymore."

That's when it sinks in. They've all marked me as their mate. Possibly more than just these four.

And they're fucking furious about it. Mating with the outcast no one wants apparently wasn't one of their life goals. They see me as a weakness, and now a threat.

"He'll make your life hell if you don't go," the blond boy urges. "I can't watch him kill you slowly."

"Get the fuck out of here," Calvin hisses at me. "Get out. You're safer if you leave."

Bea nods, and my heart drops.

I knew I was safer out of the pack. I knew I didn't belong. It just hurts to hear it spoken out loud.

Kyvain leaps to his feet.

Adrenaline spirals through me. I climb the fence once more. A big hand catches my foot, but I kick him off. When I reach the top, I flip him off one last time, a sweet goodbye to my fated mate. My battered heart soars as I land steadily on two feet on the other side.

I don't wait. I don't look back. I hurry away from the edge of the pack's territory and head toward the mountains I've always been warned to stay away from. Apparently, they're dangerous, but they're nothing compared to the danger I would face if I stayed.

Once I'm out of sight, I slow down, taking a moment to let everything sink in.

I press my palms to my eyes, and immediately feel a wave of heat in the night that continues to grow colder. Pulling my hands away, the first thing I see are a pair of ashen boots in the snow.

Because of course I've been found. I'm just that lucky. Thinking I could get away from men who can randomly materialize was an impossibility I'd only tricked myself into believing.

My gaze drifts up the man's perfect body, and kind but tormented blue eyes meet mine once more.

"Let me take you to your mother. I promise I won't harm you." He nods toward the towering blond giant of a man behind him. "I won't let Aric or Torben lay a hand on you either." Latham's honesty is a vivid thing. I can see it in the sharp features of his face, but I can feel it too.

I believe him.

Mostly because he's just the lesser of two evils.

"Or Loki," I add.

He shakes his head and releases a long sigh. "I wish you'd change his name," he says under his breath and I'm surprised how easily he makes me smile. "I'll keep the hellcat safe too."

My smile only grows wider, but it slowly occurs to me that someone's missing.

"Where *is* Aric?"

Latham motions toward the fence I left behind just as a roar of fiery rage shakes the ground I stand upon.

"Said he wanted to take care of something before

we go," Latham explains casually.

Another roar and a masculine scream cries through the night.

And once more I'm surprised by the smile these manic men bring me.

Chapter Ten

The Ice Mountains

Rhys

Torben leads us to the north, and after ten minutes of hiking through the snow, Aric jogs up to our side. I peer at him out of the corner of my eye.

His tawny hair is messy and disheveled. The jeans he wore earlier no longer have tattered tears from where Loki attacked him. He's changed into clean black jeans and a black tee-shirt. I look at him closer, but I don't see a single speck of blood anywhere on him.

A gurgling sound rumbles through his chest before a quiet noise escapes him… a burp.

"Excuse me," he says with a half-hearted smile.

His long, tattooed fingers swipe around his mouth like he can still remember the mess that was once there.

I stare at the psychopath.

He smiles at me, happy and jovial after the deathly screams I heard on the other side of the fence.

"The girl's okay, by the way," he tells me when he seems to realize I'm not sharing his keen amusement. "Walked her home myself," he adds.

It does calm my nerves a little to hear that. Everyone else, all four of my apparent mates can go fuck themselves, but it is nice of him to reassure me about Bea.

"Thank you," I whisper as we walk further up a hill.

A quietness surrounds us, but Aric stays by my side. I wish I could say it's comforting to have him so concerned over my wellbeing, but really, I'm afraid he might lash out at a deadly fly and accidentally slit my throat with his raging animalistic strength.

Aric has two sides to him it seems. And both are concerning.

An hour slips by with me on edge as I follow the three men of Hell blindly past the pack of mountain wolves who are allies to my—I mean the Dark Moon's—pack and even further into the unknown. I've never been this far from home before. I've also never seen snow falling in such big dollops of flakes like this.

A shiver races through me despite how hard I hold my arms around myself. Cold breath wafts around my face with every heave I release, and every slip of my boots against the several inches of slush makes me fight for balance.

Latham's arm locks around mine suddenly, and he holds me up against the extreme slant. I look at him, and with a wave of his hand he extends a thick black coat to me. Meanwhile, the three of them remain in tee-shirts, completely unaffected by the weather around us.

His hand is warm against my hip. He takes my bookbag and peacefully purring cat while he steadies me as I slip into the soft material. Long fingers catch at the hem, and he carefully zips me up, his hand sliding quickly up my stomach, my breasts, and collarbone in a single fluid movement.

"Thank you," I breathe out in a puff of white frost.

His pretty ice-blue eyes hold mine. The simple weight of his alluring gaze sinks through me with a tremble of reckless emotions pressing at my chest. A spark of my magic stings the air, and I have to look away before I assault him with the strange magic I sometimes expel without even trying. Now is not the time to make someone feel good. My magic has helped me ease people's anger toward me over the years, but it's also been known to cause the occasional four hour erection from time to time. Although all three of these men are deadly beautiful, and I'm sure their cocks are just as nice to look at, I need to be careful what I reveal about myself to them.

I still can't trust them.

I take a single step and my foot slides right out from under me. I stagger back but someone catches me… with two firm hands… right on my ass.

"Shit, sorry." Aric drops his hold on my cold cheeks and my weight rushes into him instantly. His chest collides with my back and then he's all around me. He tries to push me upright, but his palm slides against my back and cups the side of my boob awkwardly. His arms flail at my sides to find a platonic place on my body. "Fuck," he hisses. "Motherfucking snow in the middle of fucking California."

A big palm snatches my wrist and flings me forward, barely letting me find my footing as a glare is tossed down at the still cursing man behind me.

"Keep up. It'll only get worse from here," is all Torben grumbles out before walking away from me and continuing up the jagged, icy trail.

He's guarded. I see it in his quietness and I see it in the space he keeps between not only me, but also the two men who should be his companions.

No. I won't be getting any help from Torben if my life is on the line during this trip.

Latham and Aric stay at my sad pace despite their leader becoming a blur within the thick, windy snowfall.

Something tingles over my skin, and I'm not sure if some sort of magic or the growing cold is to blame. Either way, my nose is downright rosy, my fingers are frozen, and it's growing even harder to trudge through the deepening snow and slippery ice.

"Can't we use your weird magic to travel?" I

question as my teeth chatter from the chill. Having a shortcut would make this so much more bearable.

"Our magic won't support us carrying another person outside the Realm of the Living," Latham informs me apologetically, eyeing my chattering teeth like he can't fathom being cold enough to physically shiver.

We're not in the Realm of the Living any longer? Fuck. What have I gotten myself into?

I almost question it, but Aric mutters something about barriers, realm magic, and fucking rules. It doesn't make sense to me, but I believe them. If there was an easier way to travel than hauling my sorry ass up this mountain, I have no doubt they'd do it.

My conversation dies to nothing but exerted, gasping breaths, but I never stop moving. My future might be at the top of this mountain, and I won't give that up. I won't give up the chance to find my mother after all these years.

I can't even remember what she looked like. It's like a blank space is there when I try to think back to my life before I joined the Dark Moon Pack. She doesn't exist at all to me. Sometimes I think I still remember her voice.

But what if that's just a part of my mind trying to comfort me after all these years?

I shake my head at the pathetic thought and focus on the journey ahead.

"Where do we go once at the top?" I yell from over the howling wind.

"What?" Aric mouths, but I can't fully hear him.

"I said—"

A blade of white ice slashes through the storm. It slices into my arm with searing pain that steals my breath away before the blade flings back up. It arches to come down even harder. Aric darts out and he pummels the attacker to the ground, both of them being eaten up by the thick flurries in the dark.

I turn toward Latham but…

He's gone.

Cold hands meet my chest and it's only then that I see him—a monstrous man, several feet taller than Torben, looms over me. Jagged icicles dangle from his beard, and dry gray eyeballs look down on me as bony white fingers wrap around my neck.

"This is no place for the living," he croaks like glass as ice fills his throat.

My fist collides with his chest, but my fingers slip right through. Rib bones crack against my forearm, and for a second, I'm stuck within him. I slash against his gigantic body and his frail, tattered torso breaks apart around my arm like shattered ice.

Scrambling to my feet, I glance around with widened eyes. Latham stumbles into me, his fiery swords slashing at the attacking corpse in front of him. There's no time to think, so I act instead. Kicking out, my boot collides with the leg of the attacker and his femur makes a sickening crack that echoes off the stone mountain pass surrounding us.

The giant skeletal man falls to the snow with a

coarse scream that pierces the night. With a slash of strength, Latham drives his blade through the large skull of the thing withering on the ground. A nasty crunching sound follows every inch the sword sinks in.

"Ice giants," he tells me. "They guard this realm."

"Right," I say blankly just as another descends on me.

I fling it off before it can fully grip my bloodied arm. It tumbles down the mountain behind me,

but another rises in its place. Latham's attack sends the giant staggering backward against the slick ground, but it takes Latham with him, the snowfall overtaking my friend and washing the last image I see of him away into the night. I lunge forward at the man of bone standing before me, but two more of the skeletal giants leap onto my backpack, earning themselves a harsh meow from the sleeping cat inside.

Just as I shake one of them off, two more dig their bones into my flesh as they drag me down into the cold blanket of snow. I try to escape with slamming fists and kicking feet. The wolf inside me growls to life, but I can't focus on her. I can't focus on the strength of her magic enough to bring her forward through all my chaotic emotions. Finger-like claws scrape at my skin. Bony limbs flail over me. Cold weight presses down on me.

It's all too much.

Green eyes meet mine from over the icy skulls of the giants. Torben stomps hard, and a flash of fire erupts around us. A blaze of flames circles out from

his enormous body, igniting the walking corpses as they stagger off, wailing into the night. The ones on top of me scatter like bugs, and the godlike man stares down at me like a true savior. The snow whips at his long, messy blond hair. Snow clings to his beard. He looks untouchable.

His big hand lowers to me.

A breath slips into my lungs for the first time in what seems like an hour. I take his hand. Warmth spreads through my fingers and up my arm until it sears through my chest like magic. My lips part to ask him about his power…

But his eyes widen suddenly. His mouth drops open. And then he falls into me like a mountain collapsing. His weight pins me to the cold ground. A long blue sword made of lethal ice sticks out of Torben's back.

And the largest giant I've yet seen stands over him.

"This is no place for the living!" he crackles.

And then they all surround me.

***

My arms ache from where the giants drag me through the snow. Spindly fingers dig into the wound on my upper arm, leaving a chill that goes bone deep. Undeniable power pours from them like rhythmic lapping waves. I shiver from the feel of it as much as I do from the swirling snow. The magic they possess crawls like ants across my flesh until all I want is the hottest shower so I can scrub myself raw and wash their touch down the drain.

Behind me, one of the ice men haphazardly carries my bag while angry, mewling sounds from inside where Loki is stashed away. The strange men who have infiltrated my life called him my guardian, and I can't help but wonder if he's biding his time now, or if he even feels the danger we're stuck in. My cat is apparently much more badass than I ever knew, but I doubt he has a death wish.

Loyalty only goes so far. I shouldn't be shocked. It's a hard lesson I've learned my whole life.

Everyone I've ever known has let me down. As much as I want to know about my birth mother, she abandoned me when the only thing I needed was her. She's alive and wants to see me, but she must have given me up for a reason. I spent countless years waiting for her to come and save me. To take me away. To give me the loving home I could have had. But that was only a young girl's dream.

No. The only person I have who loves me is Bea, and our friendship just went from ride or die to *it's complicated.*

You're loved more than you know… The sweet melody of that mysterious woman's voice fills my ears, but it doesn't bring comfort and peace the way those words are meant to.

It brings pain instead, and frustration. Exhaustion even.

Loved? Please. I'm nothing more than a lone wolf now. A rogue. And now I'm a prisoner of the fucking ice giants.

So much for the pack and family. Mary is probably

rejoicing that I'm gone. Her loyalty always had an expiration, and my 'best by' date passed long ago.

Everyone has a line in the sand they're unwilling to cross.

I'm all for independence, but having no one in your corner is a lonely place to be.

My mind immediately conjures up images of the three mystery men—Latham, Aric, and Torben—but they can't be any better than the people I've been subjected to my whole life. So far they've helped me on this journey, but only because it's their job. If it comes down to me or them, I know they'll choose themselves. And I accept that.

It's up to me to get myself out of the mess I'm in. No one else will do it for me. I'm the only one I can fully depend on.

My gaze darts to the injured form of Torben. He's nothing more than deadweight that some of the smaller giants jostle in their feeble attempt to get him along the steep path they're leading us up. I half expect their skeletal forms to collapse in a heap from the struggle.

A mirthless smile curls the edges of my lips that they have to deal with his heavy ass. It serves them right for stabbing him with the icy sword that still protrudes grotesquely from his back.

Worry swirls in the pit of my stomach, but I swallow it down. Torben may be hurt, but his powerful magic still fills the air.

I take that as the small comfort it is. He'll probably be okay. Maybe. I hope…

Funny how much I care about a complete stranger. But he's *my* complete stranger. For now, that's enough.

The tall pillars of an ancient-looking temple come into view through the flurrying snow that's growing heavier by the minute.

I'm almost glad when we finally reach it for no other reason than needing a reprieve from the cold.

That is… until I'm dragged in front of the largest skeletal creature. He stands like a tower against the flurrying winds. His jaw wrenches open and expels a hiss into the night.

"Earthly belongings have no place here."

Ivory bone tries to slip under the hem of my shirt and pry the fabric up over my stomach in an attempt to undress me. No fucking way, thank you very fucking much.

I kick at the cold clawing bones that bite into my stomach, ribs, and breasts. My eyes clench closed as the ripping of fabric sounds through the night. The coat Latham gave me is tossed aside before more tears pull away in ribbons of cloth. My teeth grit hard. I curse them and kick them, but it's all over in a matter of seconds.

The giants don't take no for an answer, and soon my clothing lies in tattered shreds around my feet. Cold wind makes my nipples peak, and chill bumps break out all along my skin like tiny mountain ranges.

My cheeks are stinging pink when the monsters once again grab my arms and yank me forward.

A heavy magical barrier sits at the entrance of the temple, a luminescent veil that can barely be seen. They jerk me forward and the curtain of magic caresses my skin as they drag me through it. They all stare daggers at me like their magic is a pass or fail test, and they're waiting for the outcome.

My eyelids fall closed hard. I'm shit at testing, it'll reject me. I'll be left out in the cold to freeze into an icy corpse.

The magic rushes over me in a barrage of tingles. It slips by in an instant, and nothing bad happens… at least… I don't think.

I pass.

The harsh expressions they all wear ease the smallest amount as they glare down at me. I can see that walking through the barrier and coming out on the other side passes the invisible test I had no time to study for.

Everything's fine.

The monstrous man carrying my bag strides through the magical barrier, except something snags him. His arm jerks back and he falls to the ground in a billow of snowy air. Long, bony fingers scratch over his skull, confusion seeming to seep into him. Until he settles his sights on my backpack.

Shit.

A drum of noise consumes my ears as my heart pounds harder to see the giant stand once more, his attention on the bag as he takes a deliberate step forward. Just to be slammed back into the snow once more from the simple but strange weight of my bag…

Loki can't enter here…

Why?

The giant roars, standing quickly and rushing the veil. A meow of annoyance crawls through the silence as the two of them are thrown to the ground, and this time anger lines the asshole's deathly features. His claws rip open the bag, and he shakes the contents out. A wad of shirts and jeans as well as my infamous hot pink panties topple out and land with a suspiciously heavy plop in the thick snow.

I watch that spot with wide eyes.

Don't move. Don't move. Don't move.

The giant tosses the bag into the wind before striding through the barrier with ease. A breath slips from my lips, and it's the first sigh of relief I've had the entire fucking day.

Loki's fine. Everything's going to be okay.

A scream of agony echoes off the marbled halls in direct contradiction to that thought. It's a deep and rumbling sound, but I know instantly who it is. Icy sweat dots Torben's panting body as they forcefully drag him, a creature of Hell, through the magical veil.

And he doesn't pass their test.

Chapter Eleven

All the Swords

Rhys

Torben is completely and utterly naked.

Don't look. Don't look. Don't look.

Despite the fact that I passed the test that allowed me an uneventful entrance into what they're calling a holy temple, I'm no saint.

My gaze tracks along the dips and curves of his prone body. Scars mar his sides. Pale lines of wounds long healed rip up his arms and throat, even though it's all just rugged beauty. Torben is gorgeous. A god in his own right. A majestic, powerful creature.

It's why I'm confused as to why he's still passed out cold.

They toss us into barred cells like dogs. Torben

needs help, but they do nothing more than slam his face off the frost kissed floor before slamming the door on him. My eyes flit to the icy sword that's still sheathed within his body like it's a permanent part of his anatomy now.

It looks painful, the jagged edges gleaming in the dim light like broken glass. Blood wells around the wound, but it's slowed now. I can only hope the blade is stabilizing anything vital that may have been hit.

I crawl across the gleaming, frozen floor and press myself into the bars made of the hardest ice that secure us in our own cells. The outside walls are made of stone, but everything inside is ice and snow, as if they repurposed the room to fit their needs. I never would have pegged the ice giants for having a dungeon below their place of peace and worship, but tonight has proven that I don't know much about the world outside the bubble of the pack I grew up in.

My worldview has been broadened, and I have a feeling I've only seen the tip of the iceberg.

But I can't think about what else is left for me to discover. A shit ton, I'm sure. If I survive this frozen hellhole.

My bare tits squish against the bars as I stretch through them, trying to reach Torben, and I swear my nipples are glacial diamonds by now. I almost pray he doesn't wake up and see me like the snow cone stripper these giants have turned me into.

The edge of my fingers just graze his cold, clammy skin. The light hair on his arm abrades my fingertips. The half-giant has a patch of dark chest hair in that

sexy bear kind of way.

I press my lips into a thin line and try to jostle him enough that he'll wake up.

"Torben," I whisper, afraid if I speak too loudly, we'll draw attention back to ourselves. The ice giants have left us alone for the moment, but I doubt my luck will last.

An eerie chill whispers through the room and the hair on the back of my neck stands on end. It feels like we're being watched, but a quick glance around shows the large room is still empty. It's just the two of us.

Or is it? I don't even know anymore. After watching Latham and Aric disappear in bursts of flame or shadows, anything is possible.

The thought only makes me strain harder.

"Torben!" I say quietly but harshly. "Wake. The. Fuck. Up!"

I can't do more than gently shake his arm. It's not enough. Biting my lip, I pinch some of his arm hair between my fingers and yank. If there's one thing girls know, it's the pain of hair removal.

The sharp attack against his arm hair unfortunately doesn't work. A quiet grunt is all I get in response. I try again. Then again. If I keep going, he's going to end up with a bald patch on his arm.

And he's too pretty for any kind of early balding.

It doesn't seem to be working anyway.

Fuck.

I ease back to sit in the middle of the cell and draw my knees up to my chest. My ass practically freezes to the floor, but I ignore the sting of cold and wrap my arms around my legs. Closing my eyes, I find my focus.

I only have one idea left, and I have no clue if it will work.

But I'm not going to die here knowing I didn't try every possible solution.

The magic inside me responds to my call and I let it build. I've never openly called on it before, it just happens. So this is new.

The familiar warm and light feeling wells inside my chest, and I push it toward Torben with everything I have.

I don't dare open my eyes when I hear him grunt again. I'm not about to break the spell and fuck this up. More and more magic leaves me until Torben groans, then I hear the distinct scraping sound of a body shifting in the cell beside mine.

More. I need more.

Wake. Up!

My magic responds along with the growl of my wolf. She lends me strength until I'm overwhelmed with the feeling. The next burst of energy that escapes my chest shakes the room. Small stones and debris come loose from the ceiling and walls, falling to the frozen ground around us like dusty rain.

I scramble to the chilled bars, holding onto them as hope flares brighter in my chest.

"Fuck," Torben curses as he pushes himself up to his knees.

My gaze flies to his, and then I nearly choke as it immediately falls to an entirely different kind of impressive sword.

I'm happy to see him alive and well, but he's *really* happy to see me.

And that really says something, given how fucking freezing it is in here.

The man blinks, and then his gaze falls down my body in a slow, devouring look. The hard length of his impressive cock is all I can see, and it jumps against his abdomen as more power leaks from me even though I try to rein it back in.

"Fuck," he growls again, but this time more reverently. He's staring right at me, speaking *about* me.

It's like he's never seen a naked woman before. That can't be right. I mean… just look at him. He looks like Thor minus the hammer… unless you count the one between his legs.

Long blond hair hangs loose around his shoulders, his muscles ripple as he stands slowly. I follow him up, pulling myself to my feet using the bars that separate us.

More magic slips out of me, zapping between us like an electric current.

Lust blazes in Torben's eyes, hot enough to melt our icy cages until they harden to steel.

"They hurt you." His growl is guttural. If Latham and Aric hadn't told me he doesn't shift, I'd have guessed there was a deadly creature lurking just under his skin, glaring out through his angry green gaze.

I'm so thrown off it takes me a minute to blink and assess my arms. Hard lines of dark bruises mar my pale skin, standing out in harsh rebuke. Tacky blood dries against my flesh where a wound is slashed into my bicep. Now that I'm focusing on it, it stings like a bitch.

"I'm okay," I promise. "I've had worse." The shrug I give only makes the raging storm inside him more visceral, so I quickly change the subject. "You're hurt a lot worse than I am."

Torben tries to peer over his shoulder at the sword I motion to, but he can't see it. Craning his hand back, he reaches for the hilt.

"What are you doing?" My nakedness is forgotten as I scold him.

"Taking it out," he grumbles roughly, like I'm nothing but an annoying peasant he has to explain sword shit to.

"It might be the only thing keeping you alive!" I eye the wound, noticing the trickle of water melting from where it's embedded inside him. "It could have hit a lung, or an artery or something." I'm trying to dredge up images from old anatomy textbooks, figuring out just how bad this really is.

I'm not a doctor, I can't save him if he starts to bleed out. Fuck, I can't even save myself from this fucking frozen bird cage I'm in.

Torben eyes me like I'm ridiculous. "I'm not that breakable, princess."

The last word to roll off his tongue comes out derogatory, and though I've been called far worse, the

way he says it makes it dirtier than all the others.

"Don't call me that," I grit out. I hate the way he makes me feel insignificant when I know for a fact they wouldn't have come all this way to get me if I was just another human… or even just another shifter. They want me for a reason. One I'm still trying to suss out.

There's no way in hell they came all this way just to deliver a message from my long-lost mother or act as my bodyguards to return me to her. The story is deeper than that. I just need to dive in to find out how much.

But I can't do any of that if he's dead. Which brings me right back to the dilemma we're in.

Torben's eyes narrow like he just read my thoughts, word for fucking word.

Hell, I wouldn't be surprised if that was one of his superpowers. Stranger things have happened today.

Torben stalks closer to the bars, and I swear he's even bigger than Aric, something I thought was impossible until I saw Torben… and even the skeletons made of ice and bone that tower above us all.

I swallow as his scent wafts toward me. It's rich and sinister. He smells like a dark forest with warmer hints of fire and musk. The earthy scent drives me toward him, my wolf yearning to get even closer.

For some reason, she likes each one of these dangerous assholes.

But she is a bit unstable like that.

Two feet from the bars, he turns and presents me with the perfect view of his tight ass. Appreciation for his toned physique is all I'm paying attention to when he arches a thick, blond brow at me over his shoulder.

"Pull it," he grumbles quietly.

"I'm sorry… what?" I stumble over my words, wondering if he wants me to reach around him and…

"The sword," Torben replies dryly, like he's dealing with an idiot.

It's not my fault he blinded me with his Viking body and… other unspeakable things. My wolf is practically humping his leg, and my lady bits are all kinds of awake. I shake my head and focus.

"Yeah. No. I'm not pulling that out." I shake my head and cross my arms over my chest, well aware that the motion is pushing my breasts up and out more than usual.

Torben's not immune, either. He notices me just as I notice him.

Who's all high and mighty now?

"If you won't, I'll do it myself. But you have a better angle that won't cause further injury." He speaks the words slowly, like I need help understanding his logic.

Which is rather good logic…

"And if you bleed out?" I question, because it's a very real possibility.

"I won't."

I shake my head, but what choice do I have?

With an angry sigh, my fingers close around the

hilt and the ice stings my palms.

"On three," I whisper to him.

His response is simply a brooding look he tosses at me from over his shoulder.

I roll my eyes at the asshole.

"One," I say slowly, and his shoulders stiffen. "Two." I eye him closely as he tenses hard.

Then I yank the damn sword out of his back.

"You said three!" he groans.

"I lied."

Torben's shoulders hunch, and I know he's stifling a grunt of pain that tries to escape up his throat. The wound is raw and red. Blood seeps to coat his skin, dripping down his taut muscles to splatter on the ground.

It doesn't look good, and every fear I had comes swarming back.

My hands shake, and I drop the sword. It shatters into a thousand shards of sharp ice, but I don't spare it another glance. The power inside of me rises again, the force of it stealing my breath as my wolf's howl deafens my ears from the inside out

On instinct, I cover his injury. The bloody wound spans the entire length of my hand, from fingertip to the edge of my palm. Warm magic surges from me into Torben's body without a conscious thought.

A string of curses I don't recognize flow off his tongue as his skin knits together and his body heals before my very wide, extremely surprised eyes.

Without any warning, Torben tenses and jerks as

my magic crescendos, and the sexiest moan leaves his lips. The deep, rich timbre of it shivers down my spine and settles low in my belly. My breasts always feel heavier when I'm turned on, and the weight of them feels like it intensifies as my nipples pebble tighter. Thighs squeezing together, I let my fingers trail down his back in a light, exploring caress.

Questions bombard me, daring to ask what the fuck I'm doing, but I shut them down. I don't want to question this. Not right now. Maybe not ever.

Is it really so unbelievable that I'd be attracted to a man who could have walked straight out of an Avengers movie? This is the most explainable part of my entire unexplainable day.

With my fingers tracing back up over the newly healed skin, I try to find any sign of his previous injury, but it's entirely gone, not a scar in sight.

Holy shit. *I* did that. My *power* did that.

Torben trembles beneath my touch, a breathy groan shaking his frame.

Air heaves into his lungs before he turns with an accusatory glare darkening his eyes until I can barely see the jade I know is in there somewhere.

Feet scraping against the hard, frozen floor, I back up a step.

His tone is as dark, threatening, and deadly as an impending storm. "What the fuck did you just do to me?"

Chapter Twelve

Happy Little Accident

Rhys

I gape as I notice the cum painting the hard cut of his abs. It drips down the valley of his stomach, and I have to force myself to look away. It isn't sexy... I mean... It *shouldn't be* sexy anyway. Torben sports a semi that's still more impressive than any human or shifter I've ever seen.

Not that I've seen many.

"I... I barely touched you." My defense is weak. Obviously I did *something*. The evidence of his release gleams on his skin like an erotic picture. "I was just trying to help."

"Just keep your hands and your *magic*"—the word snaps out with the force of a whip— "to yourself. I don't need your *help*." Suggestion coats the last word, like I wrapped my lips around his cock rather than healed the wound bleeding all over the floor.

My thighs shift with an ache spreading deeper, but I ignore the needy feeling as I glare at him.

"Don't worry." I hope my gaze cuts into him as harshly as I intend. "Next time I'll just let you die."

"I'm immortal, princess."

I… fuck. What do I say to that? I didn't know, but it seems painfully obvious now. Of course these men are immortal. Why not? They're not only hot, powerful, and scary as hell… they get to live for-fucking-ever.

That seems fair.

I fume as I pace in my cell, shaking every single icy bar to test for weakness. They're solid and magic pulses through them… which totally kills any escape plan I had. Even the strength of my wolf won't be able to bash through the magically reinforced cages that holds us.

I shiver, my pale fingers starting to take on a blue hue that can't mean anything good.

Unlike the asshole next to me, I'm a mere mortal, and dying of hypothermia doesn't sound like a fun way to go.

I catch Torben's entire exterior soften as he takes in my pallor. It's then that I realize this man has layers. I'd bet my measly life savings that there's more to the story of why he's upset than he's letting on. It begs the question, what would make him upset about a magic induced orgasm? Seems like most guys beg for release.

And it was clearly an accident that I feel like a jerk for having caused.

Torben suddenly seems hurt and angered all at the same time.

And now I'm insanely curious.

I want to know, but I don't dare ask.

Torben tests each of his own bars before trying out his brand of magic. I saw the fiery blasts he's capable of earlier, but now only smoke and the smallest sparks flare from his hands.

A menacing growl cuts through the air.

"The blade was made of their holy water," he grumbles angrily as my dream of breaking out of here dies a slow death.

"What does that mean exactly?" I ask, but I already know.

"It cancels my Hell magic until it's out of my system. Enough of it must have melted into me while it was lodged in my back." Torben drives his hand into his hair, tugging on the long strands with a lost look in his eyes. "I promise I'll figure out a way to get you out of here," he says without the rough edge in his tone, more protective than combative now that he's coming off the high of anger.

Almost like he actually cares. I don't know if I should trust it.

I pace back toward the bars that connect our cells together, my hands trembling from the cold. "I didn't mean to do anything to... you know... turn you on or get you off or whatever. I... I'm really sorry," I stammer awkwardly, forcing my gaze not to travel to the mess that's drying across his hard stomach.

I want to clear the air since we're going to be stuck with each other for the foreseeable future, but he only stares at me, clearly not expecting the white flag of surrender. For a long moment, he searches for the truth in my face as well as my words.

"You don't know how to use your powers." It's a statement, not a question. He knows. Somehow, he sees the truth easily enough.

"In case you haven't noticed, I barely knew I had other powers before you all dropped into my life and turned it upside down." It's a half-truth for many reasons.

I've always been different, and I've always known that. The power living in me has grown with time, though I have no idea what it is or how it works. For the first time in my life, I have to face facts.

"I'm not a shifter, am I?" The words slip out softly, a whisper that says I'm not sure I really want the answer.

Torben gives it to me anyway. "You obviously shift." He shrugs one broad shoulder, and then crosses his arms across his golden chest. His brooding brows smooth slightly when he peers down at the crescent moon mark highlighting my chest. "But no. You're not a shifter in the sense that you're asking about."

"What am I?"

Exhaling, Torben scratches at the blond scruff on his face.

"That's not information I can give you."

"Why the fuck not?" A plea sits heavily in the cursed question. I don't understand.

Torben sighs, but it's the I'm-totally-put-out-by-you kind of annoyed exhale.

"We don't know many facts about our targets. Latham's levelheaded. He's trusted with information more. He would know. It's up to Latham to make that call of what you're allowed to know. I'm just the hired help. Think of me as your bodyguard, princess."

If he 'princesses' me one more fucking time I'm going to do more than just make him come all over himself next time.

"You don't sound too happy about the chain of command," I point out, pushing for more answers.

"Latham and I have a… history." He leaves me dangling on that cliffhanger as if I'm not totally invested now. He's no better than some of my favorite romance authors ending their books in the worst place, making me immediately buy the next book while I curse at my kindle.

"Where are Latham and Aric anyway? Do you think they know we're here?" Maybe they'll come for us… maybe—

Torben dashes my hopes again. "They'll have figured it out by now," he muses. "But there's nothing they can do for us in here, princess. We're on our own." He arches a brow as soon as my lips part. "If you thought my entrance in the holy temple was bad, it would flay Latham and Aric alive, peeling the skin from their bodies only to put it back and start all over again."

The picture he paints is grotesque, and I swallow down the bile that's risen to scald the back of my throat. Yet it begs the question, just how different is Torben from Latham and Aric that he can—albeit painfully—enter this place when they can't? And just how different am I that all I felt was a tingle upon entry to the temple?

When it's apparent he's not going to elaborate more, I sigh and try to massage the tension out of my neck and shoulders.

Either way, we're on our own.

Great.

I try to focus through the chattering of my teeth, but I don't get time to hash out a second escape plan because the door at the far end of the room opens with an ominous creak and the icy monsters walk through one at a time.

I temper my reaction to jump as the giants file into the room.

Torben growls, prowling in front of the bars of his prison like he can kill each and every single one of our enemies with the force of his glare alone.

I roll my eyes. Posturing won't help us at this point.

My cocky attitude dips, however, when one of the giants flicks his long, bony fingers and the ice that separates us melts to puddles at my feet. Heart thundering in my chest, I swallow, and despite the fact that it shows my weakness, I slash a worried look at

Torben who's seething as his gaze flies between me and the frosty giant. The chill of glacial eyes never leaves my naked form.

"It is time for the cleansing."

"I'm good, thanks." The sharp edges of my nails bite into my palms as I clench my fists. I'm nearly over the fact that I'm naked, rolling with it rather than being self-conscious of my body on display for so many people, but the vulnerability I'm left with doesn't flee so easily. I have no weapons to fight with, no way to protect myself. Unlike the bone and ice the giants are made out of, my flesh is easily harmed.

I hate to admit I'm at a disadvantage, but I'm not likely to come out of this without injury… or… you know… alive.

This was not how I pictured my death.

I mean… it's not like I had it planned out, but I hoped it'd be less humiliating than being stripped naked and accidentally making a sexy, hot Viking come on himself before being tortured by skeletal giants in a holy temple.

Yeah… not exactly how I would have planned my final moments, but it is what it fucking is, I guess.

"Please. Just let us go. We were only passing through." The plea falls flat, and I see the moment my time is up.

Lunging forward, the giant man grabs hold of my arm again and yanks me forward, making me stumble and try to catch my balance before he's dragging me across the icy floor. With another jarring grip, I'm dangling from one arm as he boldly removes me from the cell I should be all too happy to escape.

"Get your fucking hands off of her," Torben warns, suddenly much more possessive of me than he was a moment ago when it seemed he couldn't wait to get away from me. He should be happy. This 'princess' is no longer his responsibility.

The men ignore him completely, and the hellfire spitting from his eyes tells me he's not used to being dismissed.

These assholes have done more than strip him bare. Whatever holy water they injured him with has disabled his magic... or at least temporarily suspended it. They made this godlike being vulnerable, clearly uncovering a weakness even he didn't realize he had.

His growl bounces off the old stonework and the cage rattles when he throws his substantial strength into the glacial bars. The room shakes from his force.

But it's no use. Without his magic he's no better than a caged lion.

And I'm on my own.

I don't let him see the fear in my eyes. Or at least... I try not to let him see it.

But the way he gazes back at me, with fury and passion and so much fucking anger, tells me he's more observant than I gave him credit for. He's possessive and protective. I see it clearly now. Somehow Torben seems to be able to look into my soul with a single-minded intensity that makes me squirm.

I think I've lived my entire life without ever truly being seen. But Torben? He sees me. Every piece.

Even the ones I'd rather hide.

What he does with those pieces, however, is still a mystery. We're little more than strangers, barely acquaintances. And if the ice giants didn't make him look like a saint in comparison, I'm pretty sure he's my enemy more than he's my savior.

But beggars can't be choosers, and all that shit. Torben is the safest bet I have to get out of here.

Not that his presence is currently doing me any good.

Fear ripples off me in suffocating waves, and I only get one more glance at the predatory man roaring in his cage as I'm hauled out of the room.

My wrist aches, my body feels bruised and battered as I trip and fall on the rough stone steps that lead out of the dank basement. I'm dragged up and up until I'm shoved before the leader of the giants.

He stands mysteriously tall on a platform, just steps above me. His hand shadows across my face as he holds it over my head.

"You will be tried and found innocent, or you will be tried and found guilty. May your life be cleansed and your soul be counted." Each word reverberates back to me as it bounces off the hard, shiny marble.

And then I'm pushed to the edge of a large basin of water. A layer of ice lines the surface and I'm shoved closer and closer despite my thrashing arms and legs. I lash out at solid legs and only a single cracking of bone indicates I've hurt one of them at all.

My reflection peers up at me from the icy well of

water. Blonde hair lines my face in stringy dirty locks. Blood mars my features, looking more like ink against my blue lips. I'm shoved harder. The basin of water is larger than it appeared. It could serve as a tiny swimming pool for humans or a foot bath for the giant beings. With one hard kick, I'm thrown forward, forced over the edge.

A scream threatens to rip from my lungs, but I barely draw a breath before being shoved under the frigid water.

Ice cracks around me, slicing up my exposed flesh at all angles. A large hand covers my head and forces me down, unwilling to let me surface. The water stings at my skin as I descend lower. The last picture rolling through my mind is my own broken image, lost and battered looking.

How has my life come to this?

Somewhere I made a wrong turn, because this can't be the end I was destined for this whole time.

It just can't be.

I won't fucking let it.

My legs kick hard. I near the surface, but long skeletal fingers push to keep me under. Burning sensations explode in my lungs, and I flail helplessly while my wolf snarls and snaps, her fury barely heard above the sound of swishing water in my ears.

Pain strikes through me, my throat begging for a breath. My numb fingers fumble against many hands, but I can't surface.

I can't make it.

Hell Kissed

I am completely and utterly fucked... and not in the panty soaking, toe curling, blissed out, screaming kind of way.

Chapter Thirteen

Ash in the Frosting

Rhys

Spots break out across my vision as the lack of air sends my head into a spiral. I barely have time to think, let alone come up with a plan to get myself out of this situation before my lungs use up the last of their reserves. Nails dig into the bony fingers encapsulating my head, but they don't make a dent in the frozen assholes holding me down.

For one glorious second, my mouth breaks the surface, and I drag in the gulp of air my lungs are starving for, but then I'm thrust back under the water.

What. The. Ever loving. Fuck!

I can't think. Can't breathe. Can't so much as scream for help or mercy or curse the shit out of the murderous bastards trying to 'cleanse' me.

My head aches as my wolf growls the most menacing sound into my mind, but her strength wanes, her power feeling as numb as my lips.

I can't reach her.

Fuck. Fuck. Fuck!

Between the oxygen deprivation and the flood of magic that fills the water, my head spins dizzily.

The holy water bubbles against my skin, sending tiny tingles skating along my limbs. For every minute that passes, the magic increases until it's burning me like I've been tossed into a hot vat of boiling water.

I grit my teeth, needing to scream against the pain that's slashing like a million tiny knives slicing over my flesh. It traces its way up my legs, across my thighs, cutting over my stomach before my arms are being tortured by the same sharp torment.

Images of my life race past me, and I wonder if this is it. I'm dying. This is the movie everyone always talks about when they say 'my life flashed before my eyes.'

And what I see is almost more depressing than the fact that I'm enduring a slow, agonizing death as I drown.

Alone.

Just the way I lived.

I see Mary and Bea. I see the pack and Alpha Morganson. But mostly I see Kyvain and his friends, taking little pieces of my soul every day of my life. Their torture was slow. Each act, each bullying word carving away at me until I was left half a person. Until

I was forced to listen to my wolf and harden myself against the world. Until I was so broken by their actions that I'd come to expect their daily harassment as routine.

All I ever wanted was to belong in the world.

A pack.

Friends.

A family. That word haunts me. It's everything I want and yet nothing I have.

Maybe that's why I followed Latham and Aric and even Torben up this gods forsaken mountain with nothing more than a whisper and a prayer. Against my better judgment, I wanted to trust them when they said they'd take me to the mother I spent a lifetime wondering about.

Every year that passed lessened the hope in my chest that some day my parents would come back for me. That they cared. But with one word about my mother, the embers reignited and burned steadily... just like the candle on my tenth birthday that I refused to blow out until my mother came for me. I didn't even know if she was alive—or if she wanted me if she was—but I'd created a whole story for her in my head. The delusions we tell ourselves as children can sometimes be cruel, even when they're well intentioned. I can still see that flame flickering away as I waited, watching that candle burn to nothing but ash in the frosting.

Pale blonde hair floats around my face as my skin draws tighter and my lungs beg for a breath. My hands lower as my feet slowly stop kicking.

I drift for a tiny moment, finally finding a place where those nightmarish hands can't touch me.

I can't hold out much longer.

No. Fuck this. I'm not going out this way, and if I do, my tombstone will tell the world I went down the fighter my wolf always told me to be!

I thrash and kick and claw and swim.

My chest expands until I'm positive I'm going to explode into a million shards. Or have a heart attack first.

Fury ignites inside me, and I push myself harder.

The pulse thrumming through my veins slows as I grow warmer and warmer.

Overwhelming magic pours from me as I beg the Fates, the gods, the stars, anyone who will listen, for help.

I've been told about myths and gods my entire life.

One of them, any fucking one of them would be helpful in a time like this.

Echoing screeches hiss through the main hall of the temple. They're muted at first, growing louder the closer I draw to the surface after the many hands clawing through the water slowly disappear one by one. Energy as pure as lightning bolts through me and whips out with the force of a tornado when I emerge from the water.

My wolf nearly breaks through my skin in her eagerness to shift and defend.

It's all I can do to keep her back. With weakened arms, I pull myself from the pool and collapse onto the smooth marble.

I'm still just trying to get my lungs to stop hurting so badly, but all around me ice giants drop to the ground as all the life is sucked from their tall, skeletal bodies. Their faces bunch in horrifying screams and their gleaming bones lose their luster. Ice melts across the ground, dripping from their dying forms. Everything they've created out of snow and ice starts to disappear, running in rivers across the slick floor.

"Rhys!" Torben comes roaring up the stairs, finally freed in the chaos. "Princess!" His sharp bark is punctuated by a growl, his fist flying into one of the storming giants who tries to stop him from reaching me.

The giant cracks beneath Torben's strength, and he falls hard with a thunderous sound, but another rises in its place. The two of them are so close to me, but I can't feel any sensation in my legs or hands.

I physically tremble to help him. It only gets worse when an enormous skeletal hand lashes out, bones slicing across the patch of hair I'd just admired not long ago. Rage burns inside of me as crimson colors drip down Torben's golden chest. My magic strikes out in an instant. It doesn't make sense, but the giant screams that same dying sound, like a rabbit caught by an owl in the dead of night. It pierces me with the sharp reality that somehow I'm the one doing that to him.

Fear tangles with my rabid rage, and it booms out of my chest in waves of power.

One by one, they fall to my magic.

Silence cuts in.

Torben falls to his knees next to me. His warm palm pushes along my spine, but I can barely feel his touch as he helps me to sit up.

"Are you okay?" His jade colored gaze travels over me with dark intensity, trying to assure himself that I'm still in one piece.

"Yeah," I manage to croak past the rawness in my throat and the dull ache still left in my chest.

"Let's get you out of here." He helps me stand, but I'm slower than he is as we make our way to the entrance.

My feet give out on the last step of the podium. I hate how weak I feel. I can't feel much of anything at all from the cold, but I feel that pathetic feeling rising up in my chest.

"You're okay," he murmurs against my neck on a hot breath.

And I feel it.

I feel his words whispered across my skin in tingling waves.

Large arms band around me, one under my knees and the other a strong bar behind my back. Holding me against his chest, he makes it to the door in giant steps that would have taken me triple the energy to keep up with.

His heat washes into me, blanketing me in his hellish magic. It hurts but it's also bliss that sinks down and warms me to my core.

I've never been so happy to see the sky in my life

as we burst through the iridescent veil of the temple. Wind lashes out at me, pulling at the very breath in my lungs. He bends at the waist and holds something up. It looks like a battered piece of trash, but upon closer look...

"Loki!" I snatch the small cat from him and try my best to warm the icicles clinging to his fur. He blinks in a daze at me and lowers his little head onto my stomach.

I'll murder those big ass fuckers all over again for hurting him.

My fingers push through soft fur as reassuring purrs rumble through the hellcat. I snuggle into Torben's chest, absorbing his warmth and letting him be strong for me right now. The amount of magic or power or energy or whatever it was I expended in there wore me the fuck out, and between that and my lack of sleep, I'm practically a dead woman in his arms.

"You scared the shit out of me back there," Torben growls, the rumble vibrating against my cheek where it lies against his chest.

"Sorry," I murmur, truly needing sleep. The darkness hangs heavy over us, officially making this the longest day of my life. "I'll try not to get murdered next time."

Torben huffs a small laugh that startles me so badly I stiffen in his arms and pull away far enough to look up into his face. Thick scruff lines his angular jawline, and his long hair lightly brushes against my bare arm with every step he takes. Mirth flares in his eyes, lighting the green from jade to something so

much brighter for the briefest moment before they harden again.

I know. If I hadn't seen it for myself, I wouldn't have believed it either.

This golden god isn't as soulless as he wants me to believe.

There's something in Torben that is damaged the same as I am, and that dark part of him calls to me like a siren's song.

Who hurt him the way society hurt me?

I don't know why, but I want to rip whoever it was to shreds. I would though. He doesn't deserve this pain.

It's not hard to understand why he keeps mountainous walls in place around himself. He's guarding himself, trying to keep other people out… or maybe he's just trying to keep himself in.

I know that feeling. The one that says you won't get hurt if you don't let anyone get close to you.

For years it was easy to convince myself I was better off alone.

It's easier not to get hurt when you don't care about anyone.

It was how I survived being adopted by a pack who didn't want me. But being alone makes for a dull and lifeless existence. Bea splashed color into my monochrome existence, yet now Latham, Aric, and even Torben are adding to the canvas and promising me a masterpiece on the other side.

"It's only going to get worse from here," Torben

says, his face pinched like only part of him is truly concerned for me. There's a war playing out behind his eyes, and I wish I could decipher where the lines are drawn. Or what each side is fighting for.

"I have nothing to go back to."

The truth hangs over us like a dark cloud, but he knows I'm right. All that waits for me back down this mountain is betrayal, a pack I never truly belonged to, and the position Kyvain all too generously offered me.

"I refuse to be a whore." The softest whisper leaves my lips, but Torben hears it. His arms tighten around me to almost crushing levels, but I don't complain.

I find comfort in it, interpreting it the way I need, whether Torben means to offer me protection and solace in his arms or not.

I close my eyes as my head lolls against his massive shoulder and heat washes over me from the rapidly appearing man I know has just popped into existence.

"Oh fuck!" Torben chokes out, and I realize I must look dead in Torben's hold. "No…"

"She's breathing, you unobservant asshole," Aric helpfully replies. "Just look at her tits. They're moving."

A blush blooms in the arches of my cheeks as I realize Aric is ogling my nakedness. My gaze snaps open and levels on the smirking man with molten eyes.

I'd say Aric's a perv, but really, he's just raw. I get the feeling he doesn't get a lot of contact with other

people in Hell. He doesn't have a filter or awareness of someone who's constantly performing for everyone around them.

He's entirely himself.

And that's something I don't think I've ever seen in anyone I've ever met.

Latham hurriedly magics me a large tee-shirt that I wiggle into as best as I can while being pressed against the giant who refuses to put me down.

I hope he never does. I hope he carries me around like his lap goddess for the rest of his immortal days.

"We were trying to get in, but…" Latham's eyes darken.

Aric's glower is as dark as midnight. "The fuckers took you to the one place we couldn't go."

"Technically there are entire realms you can't go." Torben's smirk is thoroughly amused as he steals the weary eyed house cat from my arms and carefully hands it to Aric.

Aric's lips curl as he takes the thing like it might possibly explode in a fiery ball of fur if he's not careful. Honestly, Loki might. If he was fully conscious that is…

I swallow hard at that thought.

"As much as I love this bromance, can we go?" I glance over Torben's shoulder, worried those icy skeletons are going to stomp through the snow and actually succeed at killing us this time. "I'm not sure if I actually killed them or just temporarily took them out."

Aric tenses, his entire frame going into beast mode as he prepares to unleash hell on earth… or whatever fucking realm we're currently in, because it's definitely not the mortal one I grew up in.

Latham eyes Torben who nods in response, an entire silent conversation passing between them.

Probably about me.

"She's powerful," Torben replies out loud, and there's a hint of awe behind his informational tone. Though if I pointed it out, he'd never confess to it.

"Let's hope that serves her well in the future." Latham swallows, and the three men share a look I don't understand.

"Let's get to higher ground. We'll take shelter until sunrise." Torben carries me out into the darkness, and I hate that we're pausing to find shelter. All of us are beaten and bruised, but I can't help the sinking feeling in my stomach at the idea of not continuing on.

A heavy yawn overtakes me, and I lean into Torben fully, my arms draping over his wide shoulders. I accept his decision.

But only because I'm too worn and tired to oppose that decision.

I just hope I'm not making the biggest mistake of my life. Because I think I trust these psychotic assholes.

Chapter Fourteen

If You Dare

Rhys

Pain stabs through my drowning lungs and my eyes fly open with a gasp. The shitty dream fades slowly as my heartbeat returns to some semblance of normal. Darkness is still heavy in the sky as I stare out of the mouth of a cave. The sun hasn't yet fought off the night and saved me from the nightmare that is this mountain.

I lift from the frigid ground, but a warm hand slinks over my hip. That feeling drifts through my chest, filling me with magic, calmness, and most importantly, warmth. I lean back into that delicious feeling of a hot bath that the mysterious fenrir offers me.

My head tilts to the side, and I meet his starry blue

eyes. Galaxy eyes. Gray swims within the deep blue there, and I could get lost staring at this man.

"Hey, go back to sleep. You're safe here," Latham whispers while the deepening shadows under his eyes paint a story of this protective man in front of me.

I peer slowly around at the jagged walls of the cave. A small circle of embers just a foot away from me lights up the space. I don't remember coming here.

I fell asleep... on Torben.

My eyes blink slowly as that thought settles in. Twelve hours ago I didn't trust these hellions with my cat, and now I'm snuggling up and turning into Sleeping Beauty in their arms...

A lot has passed in twelve hours though.

Life and death and everything in between.

"You haven't slept." I look at Latham, judging the haziness of his gaze.

He shakes his head.

He's been watching me, watching over me like a guardian of Hell. At my feet, a different guardian of Hell rubs up against me. A small gray house cat looks up at me. Loki watches me with wide, strained eyes.

My fingers run through his soft fur, feeling the life thrumming through him as I try to forget how he looked just a few hours ago. I can't let that happen to him again. He may be my guardian, but I feel very much responsible for the ferocious hellcat.

A quiet cough shakes through the silence, and I look up to find Aric leaning into the shadows at the mouth of the cave. His silhouette is all hard angles and

curving muscles of a man who doesn't seem to fear anything.

Not even death.

I pull out of Latham's intoxicating warmth and wander toward the entrance of the cave. Wind flicks at my hair and bites at my exposed thighs where my large tee-shirt doesn't cover nearly enough. It's like Aric knows I'm cold, because the moment he spots me, he reaches out, wrapping me up in his fiery scent. He pulls me against his side, and I steal away a bit more of that hellfire warmth they hold inside of themselves.

"You should be sleepin'," he murmurs as he pulls me tighter against his body. Tattooed fingers are firm against my shoulder, like he's afraid something in the night might steal me away.

Again.

"Have you seen anything?" I ask seriously.

What if they come back? What if they find us? What if dead isn't really dead when you're already a fucking skeleton?

"No. They don't go toward the peak. They avoid the mountaintop as much as they do the base near the living." His rough tone is a reassurance, and I don't think even he realizes it comforts me.

I nod as the pressure in my chest eases.

Latham saunters over and leans against the wall near my side, his body heat spreading into me. I snuggle between the two of them, and the hype I've heard from men in my pack about threesomes finally makes sense. The body heat alone is worth the awkwardness I would surely bring to that kind of party.

"Truth or dare?" Aric asks, and my eyes fly open fast.

This isn't the kind of game that ends well. Especially with two sinfully sexy men like Aric and Latham. Or a woman who is too damn tired to care about things like pants or even underwear for that matter.

No, it ends stupidly. Someone always ends up naked running through a neighborhood, and quite honestly, I have no plans for getting naked on this mountain ever again!

I pull at the thin hemline of my shirt, but it sadly stays the same short length.

"Truth," Latham answers, skirting past my anxiety with his simple reply like it doesn't exist.

Frost kissed wind flings my hair against my face as I look up at one man and then the other.

"Is it true that wolf sex feels better than human sex?" Aric arches his scarred eyebrow at his friend as he clearly waits with intense interest on this subject.

That was... not what I thought he was going to ask. But I can't lie, I'm actually insanely curious what the answer will be.

A shy sort of smile lifts at the corners of Latham's cheeks, and a buzz of energy flits through me at how bashful the hellish man suddenly seems.

"Definitely true," he whispers in a gravelly tone that's a mix of sin and molten heat.

My thighs shift strangely, reminding me of my lack of panties.

Would it be weird if I asked Latham for a pair of underwear right now?

A pulse throbs there when those starry eyes peer down at me.

Yeah. It would be awkward as sinful fuck.

"Truth or dare, Love," Latham asks me like a promise.

A promise of naughty, terrible things to come.

Apparently this is the distraction I need to bury the shitty memories of everything that's happened tonight. They seem to know it too.

I dip my head forward and spot Torben sleeping with his back firmly against the far wall of the cave. He's sleeping off the terrible night just as he should.

As I should.

I swallow hard.

"Uh… truth," I say as evenly as my slamming heart will allow me.

Aric's fingers drift up and down my arm, calming me as well as making me completely insane by his minute touch of distraction.

"Is it true that mortal women often fake orgasms?" A line forms between Latham's dark eyebrows at how concerned he is about this issue.

My lips part, but I can feel how hot my cheeks are getting. I tip my head out from between the two of them just to let the painfully stinging wind hit my face.

I lied. Being between these two isn't bliss. I'm fucking burning up. It's too hot here now.

Way too hot.

"Um, from what I understand…" I bide my time, but every woman I've ever heard talk about it said the same thing—they didn't come. Or at least, they didn't *think* they did. "From what I understand, women like the feeling of it. It feels good to be wanted. Touched. Loved. So I guess they don't care as much about, um… actual orgasms as much as men do."

"What the fuck?" Aric hisses so loudly that a disgruntled snore echoes in the back of the cave.

The line between Latham's eyebrows is so deep now it's grown from curiosity to outright concern.

"They don't care about coming?" he asks blatantly.

I half shrug, half shake my head.

The few dates I'd been on in the past never lead to actual sex, but the fun times we did have in the back of cars and movie theaters didn't lead to an orgasm either. But it was still nice. It was nice to be with someone who actually wanted to spend time with me… to kiss me… to touch me…

Orgasm wasn't important compared to that.

"And the men, they don't care about making their partner come?" Latham's tone grows more and more outraged as he speaks.

Once more, I do that stupid shrugging shake.

"Lazy is what it is." Aric grunts. "Fucking is an event. Make her come before, and it'll be better

during. Make her come during, and it'll be even better after. And shit, make her come after and—"

"Okay! I get it. You fucking drown in orgasms, I get it!" My cheeks are so damn hot I have to shove out of his embrace and stumble into the abrupt coldness.

Both men stare at me, bewildered.

"Um." I swallow harshly, but my pussy is pulsing so hard there's clearly not any blood flow left for my brain. "Uh… truth or dare?" I swing my attention up to the cocky dragon shifter.

A smile tips his lips.

"Dare."

Of course he chooses dare.

Of course he does. He doesn't give one flying dragon fuck about streaking across the snowy mountain naked. Probably does it all the time just for a bit of exercise.

Asshole.

"Fine." I fold my arms and try to regain some control over this game.

Words flit through my mind like a grown woman playing flower girl, tossing words at me that I know I shouldn't say.

I dare you to kiss me. She tosses a few petals of ideas into my brain.

I dare you to fuck me. She scatters more merrily.

I dare you to make me come before, during, and after. She sprinkles the stupid petals all around like a raining parade of bad ideas.

My wolf practically purrs, loving the sound of each dirty, sinful thought.

"I dare you to kiss Latham," I blurt.

The grown-ass flower girl drops the basket of petals as she glares at me and the words I just spoke that don't benefit my throbbing pussy whatsoever.

Aric blinks at me in confusion, and to be honest, I'm fucking confused at myself too. Latham smirks to himself as Aric lifts his hands in what appears to be frustration in front of him. Yeah… I turned our sexy talk of wet orgasms into a dry two-man sausage fest.

I hate me too, buddy.

Latham steps forward, and though Aric seems flat-out confused about my choice of dare, he slides his long fingers through Latham's messy black hair and pulls him in good and close. My mouth falls open as the two men lock eyes, even as their lashes lower ever so slowly, the space between them slipping away with every passing second. Aric's fingers tighten as he claims the kiss. Latham's hand slides up, pushing at his friend's shirt until it lifts slightly and hard lines and inky swirls of tattoos glide beneath his palm. Their tongues meet with a single delicious flick just before their lips seal sweetly.

I think I just discovered a new part of me I didn't know existed.

My throat closes. I can barely breathe. I don't blink, not willing to miss a second, and my thighs shift against one another so hard the pressure only frustrates the neediness that's already rising.

Aric tugs lightly at Latham's inky locks as he kisses

him once more before both men pull back with a pair of slicing smiles clinging to their lips.

Deep down, I know I should close my mouth. I shouldn't leave it open and gaping as I watch the two of them like a total fucking creep. But I just can't reasonably think clearly enough to actually do it.

Then they're looking at me, still huddled close, still touching lightly as the two of them turn their heads and appraise me like I'm their next meal.

"Truth or dare?" Aric asks with a rumbling tone full of sinful want.

I somehow remember to close my mouth and take an actual breath of air.

Dare.

Dare.

Dare.

"Truth," I squeak.

Fuck!

No!

Ask for a redo! And panties, for fuck's sake!

Aric's smile is a cruel, predatory expression filled with bad, bad decisions.

"Is it true you want me to kiss you like I just kissed Latham?" His sexy, gravelly words are carefully spoken, and I can tell he simply rephrased his original dare into a truth that will screw me either way.

Yes.

The answer is a hard, irrefutable yes.

My tongue slips over my lips, and both men follow

that small movement like they can taste me just by watching. There's always been this back and forth, double-sided coin of a personality inside of me. The quietness is that little girl who was never accepted in life. The one who loved deeply but never received it in return. And the fearlessness inside of me is the wolf who wouldn't let me shrink away into the submissive servant everyone wanted that little girl to become.

I want to be the latter. I want to be her so fucking badly.

And that's all I think about as I stride forward, my steps assured and dominant as I walk right up to the intimidating dragon shifter, and run my fingers up his worn shirt to feel the hard lines of his chest underneath as I hold his taunting fiery gaze. Anxiety and recklessness run rampant within me. Even as I stretch against him as high as I can reach and hover my lips just over his.

"It's true," I whisper against him. His eyes flash with a dare. His head lowers closer. My back arches so hard my breasts meld against him. My lashes flutter. Then his tongue slides torturously slowly against mine.

He claims me with a single thrust of his fingers through the locks of hair at the base of my neck. The dominating feel of his hand takes control of my entire body as he pulls me as close as he can get me, his hard body colliding with mine in a rush of power that sparks all across my flesh. My hands slide beneath his shirt just as Latham's had moments ago, and the hot spark of his skin meeting mine is an addiction I didn't know was possible. Deeper he kisses me. His mouth

taunts mine just as much as his words always have. His other hand jerks at my hip, his fingers digging into my flesh until I'm lined up just right to feel the hard bulge beneath his jeans.

A whimper slips from my lips on a gasp of breath that my manic dragon eats right up as he consumes my lips, my tongue, the very air I breathe.

From behind me, a gentler touch skims up my waist and over my ribs before stopping abruptly at the curve of my breasts. Warm breath kisses the back of my neck as hesitant lips hover along my ear.

"Rhys," Latham rasps against my skin, his nose running the length of my jawline and down the curve of my neck.

Another needy breath hums through me as I grind my ass against the man who holds me so sweetly from behind.

"Rhys," he whispers once more, and my lashes flutter as I pull away from Aric to look into his bright, sun-kissed blue eyes.

Because the sun has risen.

The night has passed.

And that spell of complete confidence within me wanes as I realize what we have right now won't last. Not even for a minute longer.

"We have to go, Love," Latham says as his gaze dips from my eyes to my lips.

His hand is still warmly beneath my shirt, his thumb skimming the tender curve of my breast.

The air in my lungs ceases to exist.

I watch him as he studies me. Aric smooths my hair down intimately as his hands slowly fall away. The two of them steal away their delicious touch like magic dissipating in the cold icy wind.

A heartbroken look shines more than ever in the tragically beautiful gaze of the fenrir in front of me.

And then he walks away.

Chapter Fifteen

Ass Masks

Aric

Climbing the Ice Mountain has never been this hard.
And neither has my cock.

A grunt growls through me as I adjust my jeans
for the third time this morning and follow the halo of
an ass that's leading me to the top. A better man
wouldn't look.

But a better man is a bitch for missing the sight
I'm basking in right now.

The tight black jeans she pulled on this morning
cling to her curves as a heavy coat blankets nicely
around her frame. Honestly, part of me is just thankful
her lips aren't blue anymore. And the other part of
me…

I peer up at the godsend of a view above me and
adjust all over again.

Latham lingers at her side, offering her a hand here and there when she bends at the waist to get a better grip on the icy rocks. I pause every time, occasionally lifting her boot up with my palm to get her to the next handhold. My face is nearly buried in her ass each time, but it's a price I'm willing to pay. I'm a gentleman through and through.

Latham arches a brow at me after the second time it happens, but I earn a sweet 'thank you' as well as an ass mask while he just gets forgotten and a bit of hand holding as a reward.

I wink his way, but he just shakes his head and ignores me.

Or pretends to.

The wind snaps around her frost-kissed blonde hair, and she's so tired I can see it in the dullness of her blue eyes when they meet mine. She looks down at me for far too long, and I can't stand it anymore. I storm up the steep incline, and her confusion only deepens when my hands slide around her thighs and I haul her up. Her legs lock all the way around my hips as she stares down on me with parted lips.

Mmm. I like this.

I think I'll keep her here for the rest of the trip.

Until her cold hand snaps across my cheek.

"Put me down! You're going to get us both killed."

Ouch. Weird way to say thank you…

Torben stops, and the sun circles around his hard features like the gods are looking down on him and

him alone.

"Quit fucking around. We're close." He doesn't pause for us though. He just keeps going.

Latham stands tall on the side of the mountain as he watches us closely, probably picking apart what it is this pretty woman sees in my messy, manic mind. You and me both, my friend.

Most women are intrigued by me. I don't get a lot of social interaction, and I'm not about to waste it on censoring myself or tiptoeing around. They're curious, but they're not stupid enough to get too close. Fear always wins out over curiosity.

Rhys Love just doesn't have that fear inside of her to save herself from me.

And fuck if that doesn't make me want to keep her locked around my hips for the rest of our fucking lives.

I stride up the slick path, my steps even as I walk with this delicate package of a woman in my arms.

Her hands settle on my shoulders, curious eyes watching me the entire time.

"Are you and Latham more than friends?" she asks under her breath.

I chew on my lip as I try to understand her question.

"I don't even think we could call ourselves real friends, Love," I tell her, answering the best I can.

I see Latham a few times a year. We trust each other in times of need. But we don't really know each other much at all.

It occurs to me then that I don't have a single soul for a friend. My brows furrow hard, but the warming memory of my immaculate hoard of treasures back home washes out the worry of friendship.

Her pale blue eyes narrow with heavy confusion.

Shit. What was she talking about?

"You kissed as if there was more between you."

Right. Friends. And kissing apparently.

Latham doesn't look back at us, but I know he's listening. He's close enough to put that shifter hearing of his to good use.

"Where I live, I don't get any visitors. I'm alone a lot, Latham is much the same. When I do meet people, and when I find that attraction in them like—like I did last night…" I smile wide, and she blushes even harder. "I don't think. Attraction and fucking, that has nothing to do with your brain and everything to do with your heart."

I see her trying to twist that into some kind of mortal logic that makes sense.

"So you're attracted to men and women," she says slowly.

My smile only grows.

Humans thought the Earth was flat for so long that their thinking never really evolved into more dimensions than that surface level understanding.

"Men and women. And elves. Giants. Dwarves. Fucked a goddess once, but she'll never admit to it." I reminisce aloud about my hoard of memories, only to be interrupted by Latham's scowling annoyance.

"Fucking gods, he's conceited," he whispers under his breath.

What can I say, when you're right, you're right.

She's quiet for a long time, and I didn't ask in the cave but…

"Have you ever experienced it?" I ask as my gaze catches hers, and I feel that spark of her beautiful magic fire all through me.

"You mean like actual sex?" she hisses, and Latham full-on trips at the sound of her hushed words. He face-plants into the snow hard, and I don't give him a second glance when I walk past his snow angel antics.

I nod as I eat up the desire shining in her ocean eyes.

She shakes her head quietly. "I dated a few human boys in high school, but…" Her casual words drift off into that half shrug thing I've seen her do before.

I want to drop my hands and lower her against me until her hot pussy is pressed right where I want it.

But I walk on instead. I lift her higher even, to a more platonic place against my chest rather than my cock.

I have a sudden urge to shield her right then and there. I want to prevent all the shitty things in this realm and the realms to come from ever touching her.

Especially fucking human boys. Can't even remember to make their mates come. What a waste of cock.

Her pack didn't appreciate her either. Those

men—her fucking pathetic excuses for mates—they didn't know what they had.

"I-I got you something." I feel slightly self-conscious as I shift her weight to one hand to reach into my pocket.

I've never given away a piece of my hoard before. Not one single broken spoon. My collection is all I have in my home. It keeps me company to see my mementos of the places I've been and the people I've met.

But this one… it belongs to her.

Within my pocket, I slip past the dwindling ration of food from home. Then my fingers tangle with thin lacy fabric that surprises me for a second. Confusion tenses my face before realization dawns on me. Right… stole the pink panties that were blowing in the wind back at the temple…

I shove her secret stolen panties aside before finding the item I was looking for.

With a small smile, I lift my hand between us. Her eyes are bright with anticipation, and my heart soars to have her full attention.

My fingers splay open to reveal the tiny gift.

Her mouth does that thing where it falls open, but not in awe. *Is she confused? Does she not understand what it is?*

I pick up the item and hold it between my index finger and thumb.

"It's his. That little shit who tormented you," I explain and wait for her gasp of amazement and appreciation.

Hmm. She isn't gasping…

"Is that—is that a finger?" she asks with a curl of her lip.

I nod. It should be obvious. Clearly, it's his finger.

"I got it for you. The ring, I think it's his family insignia, so you'll always remember that he can't hurt you anymore."

I shove the rigid finger in my mouth and hold it there while I work the metal ring off of the fleshy end of it. She dry heaves strangely and looks away from me as I tear off the shiny ring with a breath of achievement in my lungs. I spit the finger out. It drops and sinks into the snow like a forgotten piece of memorabilia that I'll never get back, but I have to smooth over this weird disgust that's lining her pretty features right now.

She hesitantly peers back at me. I hold the now fingerless ring out to her in the palm of my hand, and her eyes brighten slightly.

Ah. So it was the bloody finger that was a turnoff.

Noted.

She takes the jewelry and holds it with both hands. The sunlight shimmers off the edge of the metal and shines across her face in an arc of golden colors.

"You killed him," she whispers.

I nod as a large smile creeps over my lips.

"For me."

I nod harder, smirking even harder too.

And then she's smiling as well.

Her attention is punctuated with a wave of warm magic that I've never felt until I met her. Her power trembles through my chest like a second pulse.

She's special.

Just like Hela said.

And I have no fucking idea how I'm supposed to finish this job now that I know that.

Chapter Sixteen

The Peak

Rhys

Aric's hard body slides against mine as he lowers me. The defined lines of his biceps are smooth against my palms. My gaze holds on the fiery depths of his russet eyes until my feet peacefully touch the icy ground. The heavy ring rests loosely against my middle finger, and even though it was Kyvain's, it was a gift from Aric.

And I'll never forget that as long as I live.

Violent wind whips around us, clawing at my hair as I look out over the world below us.

Wispy clouds cling to the edge of the mountain. Bits of green grass and blue water can be seen between them. A serene sensation falls over me. This is it. This is what heaven must feel like.

"I don't think we should take her," Aric blurts out.

All three of us turn to look at the wide, manic-eyed man.

"What?" I ask in a shaking breath.

"I said that two fucking realms ago!" Latham growls.

"We're taking her," Torben says with nothing more than a murmur of quiet authority.

"No." Aric steps toward his friend, but I note the way his shoulders square up in a less than friendly way.

Torben seems suddenly attentive to something other than the task at hand. And the glare he gives the dragon shifter is total controlled confidence.

"We have an order. We will follow through with that order." Torben speaks clearly and casually,

but just under that layer of calm, cool collectedness is a monster I can tell is rearing to rip out.

He seems every bit a shifter.

And yet he isn't...

The three of them are more than a mystery to me despite how much trust we've gained through this journey. What more are they hiding?

"Why don't you want me to go now?" I turn on him in an instant, and his molten eyes catch mine.

"Because you don't belong there," Aric answers flatly.

"I don't belong anywhere. But I'm going to find

my mother." I look from one man to the next, but it's Latham's tragic gaze that catches my attention. "My mother *is* there, isn't she?" I ask slowly.

I need answers to so much more than that, but we have to start somewhere.

A pause drifts through him, but there's an honesty in him that I'll never be able to ignore as he nods solemnly.

"Okay," I whisper, the single word coming out more clear and concise than I expected given the fast pace of my heartbeat. "Then stop acting like you're in charge of my life." I step past Aric, and I feel his attention follow me as I look up at the seven foot tall man before me. "Where to now?"

Torben's eyebrow lifts high as a surprising smirk pulls at his lips.

Until he points straight down.

I follow the direction of his index finger, but I still don't understand.

My mouth parts but then closes again as I try to process.

"You have to come up in order to get back down," Aric adds, as if that explains it all.

My mouth falls open then.

Wait.

"You've got to be kidding me," I mutter under my breath like a crazed person as I pace toward the rocky ledge of the mountain. I peer over the edge of the cliff. A strange body of water can be spotted between the thick clouds. My vision extends with the help of my wolf to get a better view of the emerald sea that crashes against the sharp jutting rocks so far below me they look like they're cast in miniature. "I am not jumping off of this!"

Words tumble out of my mouth before I murmur to myself about how I'm not this insane.

"I think you broke her," Aric none too quietly whispers to Torben, who stands near their small gathering with his feet shoulder width apart and his corded arms crossed over his chest.

I swear he's standing there to block my retreat, in case I decide to haul ass back down the mountainside and take my chances with the giants or my pack.

Now that I know Kyvain's dead, maybe it won't be so bad. Except for the tiny fact they'll probably kill me on sight for having a hand in his death. His blood's not on my hands directly, but it's definitely splattered in my direction. I literally almost held his tattered finger as a gift moments ago.

And now I'm wearing his ring...

Definitely doesn't put the odds in my favor with the Dark Moon Pack.

Latham's fingers are hooked in the pockets of his jeans. His hair hangs across his forehead in messy waves while his blue gaze tracks my every move. He's willing me not to do this, which is why I don't meet his blazing stare.

"You don't have to do this..." Latham tries, but Torben shoots him a slicing look that says otherwise.

"Why are you giving her false hope? We've been

sent to bring her back. You truly think they won't send others in our place if we fail?" the giant challenges.

Muscles in Latham's jaw jump as he clenches his teeth, annoyance and surrender bleeding off of him in tandem.

"It's not that bad," Latham says weakly, nodding to the cliff's edge.

"Think of it like bungee jumping," Aric suggests.

"Ha." The nervous, jittery sound wavers between us. "Bungee jumping without the *bungee*." It sounds even more insane when I say it out loud.

Aric shrugs like it makes no difference to him. I have a feeling that not much scares him at all.

"You have to jump if you want to get to the bridge between realms, Love. You're not just jumping into the ocean, you're jumping into a door," Aric explains more rationally.

"Sounds equally painful," I deadpan.

Aric grunts, and Latham cuts in with a rueful smile. "Think of it as a portal. You have to access the outer ring of Helheim and be granted access to the actual Realm of the Dead."

"This is the only way." Torben nods toward the edge, punctuating the end of Latham's helpful information with an immovable period.

I swallow. This is going to happen whether I like it or not. Heartbeat thundering in my chest, I pull my metaphorical big girl panties up and prepare myself.

The ledge of the mountain we're standing on kind of reminds me of Pride Rock in the Lion King, jutting out over the ocean far from where the waves crash into the shore below. But it doesn't ease the anxiety any less.

The snow flurries are just crisp cold air in the morning sunlight, but if we linger I'm sure the frigid temperatures will fall right back in.

I can't linger on this fucking death trap of a mountain any longer.

"Just… just give me a minute." I hold my hands out at them like they're going to physically tackle me over the ledge, though none of them have moved so much as an inch toward me.

Warmth nudges aside some of the panic I'm feeling as I realize all three of them are respecting my space and ability to process yet another insane turn of events.

Although Torben does so a bit louder than the others.

"You've already had fifteen minutes," Torben grumbles quietly, his complaint whipping away on the cold wind.

"Excuse me for taking a little time before I jump to my very mortal death!" I sass back.

The three men exchange another heavy look, Aric glowers hard at Torben before turning to me. The beast of a man looks like he's ready to spill the world's secrets. Instead, when he opens his mouth, all that comes out is another promise.

"I wouldn't let anything happen to you," Aric swears, brows fiercely pulled together like I should have known this already.

And I do. Or I think I do.

What is happening in my life right now? Yesterday this asshole was my enemy.

I swallow hard.

"Can't we just poof to another realm?" I wave my hand, indicating the disappearing trick they like to pull on me, hoping the answer has changed since the last time I asked. "Blaze us away, Latham."

Torben just stares at me like he's not sure how I've lived so long without common knowledge of their hellish world. I arch a brow right back, propping my hands on my hips, unwilling to back down from what seems like a perfectly logical question.

"Realm rules, Love," Latham explains apologetically. "You have to physically cross through them. It's not possible to 'poof' from one to the next, even for us. Besides, I told you our magic won't carry you outside the mortal realm."

"Lawless fucking place," Aric mutters like the Realm of the Living is somehow worse than Hell. He catches me watching him, and the corner of his lips pull up in a half smile that draws out that dimple I want to lick. It distracts me enough to make the new information I learned take an extra moment to sink it.

"Magic rules," I mutter. But it makes sense.

"You know of them?" Aric questions as Loki pounces around his feet chasing the light floating snowflakes, making himself the cutest little kitty who ever lived. It's kind of fun to see Aric take a liking to my cat. He knows how much the furball means to me, so now Loki means something to him too it seems.

Or maybe he's just a big softy on the inside. Like… *deep* inside. Past the scary exterior of that serial killer charm he holds.

"I know about them from the books I read. Every story is set around some set of magical rules that often only serve to make shit difficult." I wave a hand all Vanna White style toward the ledge I'm getting ready to leap from.

Fuck. I'm really doing this, aren't I?

"Are you ready?" Torben stomps forward, running out of patience, but there's a tension to his shoulders, a tightness he carries around with him like a new weight has settled there.

"I'm never going to be ready, so we might as well just do it." I shrug, knowing it's true.

Aric whistles for Loki, who comes trotting over like he didn't just try to kill the guy the other day. Latham twists his wrist, and a duffle bag with a soft lining appears in his hand. Aric takes it and splays it open on the ground like he's preparing a fine bed for the Queen of England or something. My cat curls up in the bag, happy for the free ride, and Aric zips it completely shut this time. Loki mewls his frustration, but it's like he knows this is the safest option, because he quiets after minimal protest.

"I'll go first," Latham offers. "That way you can see what happens. Hopefully it'll help you trust us." His confession warms me to the core. He wants to make this easier on me, and I appreciate the hell out of him.

"Okay." I nod.

With a sexy smirk and a wink, Latham walks casually past me. He strides to the edge as he faces me with that alluring look of calm confidence. Then he gracefully launches himself off the ledge.

A scream rips from my throat. I… fuck. He actually jumped! A tiny part of me thought they were joking. That they'd turn around and laugh about how they had me going. We'd walk jovially back down the mountain and have a nice brunch with the ice giants in their temple of doom.

This… this brings reality crashing down around me like sharp, dagger-esque hail.

I scramble for the edge and watch Latham dive into the churning sea.

"Your turn," Torben demands. It's clear he doesn't trust Aric to make me jump.

"Come on, Love." Aric holds out his hand and I take it.

My fingers tremble in his large grip. He's gentler now than he has been this whole time as he pulls me back a few steps.

"You're so fucking tiny. You're going to need to run to launch yourself." His gaze rakes over my frame skeptically, but I'm not a weakling. My wolf rumbles her agreement and lends me her strength, ready to show up the arrogant, sexy asshole next to me.

The challenge shores up my resolve as I narrow my eyes on him.

Smirking wickedly, he murmurs, "There she is." Then he's tugging on my hand, and I'm running next to him.

He doesn't back down. He matches me step for step, and I love that he won't let me do this alone.

I love that he cares despite how hard he doesn't want to.

Snarls bounce around inside my head as my wolf's power fills every fiber of my being. Aric's dark chuckle is all I hear as my foot breaches the edge of the cliff. Muscles bunching, I kick off the edge and propel myself into the air with more strength than I've ever possessed.

Hand in hand we jump.

A scream claws at my throat, but I hold it back. I refuse to show a single sliver of fear.

Wind rips through my hair, and the chill of the mountain freezes the breath in my lungs as the crashing waves below become a steady rhythm to set my racing heartbeat to.

I spread my arms, still holding onto Aric, whose sole focus is on watching me. I feel his attention like fire across my features. The wind becomes a caress beneath my arms as I soar faster and faster. Adrenaline torpedoes inside of me. It builds all through my body in waves.

I'm falling. I'm flying.

I'm fucking free.

Chapter Seventeen

Sharing Air

Rhys

That feeling only lasts for a little while, then terror sets in as the emerald sea grows closer.

Aric's hand tightens around mine, and we lock eyes through the strands of hair that whip wildly around my face. His gaze sears into mine as he urges me into a dive. Curving his arm around the bag that holds Loki, the large man cradles it to his chest and curls his shoulders, preparing for a much harder impact than I am.

My body tenses. Muscles coil as my eyes close tightly shut.

And then it slams into me.

A thousand tiny knives stab into every part of me when we hit. Rushing water steals all sound away, other than the stuttering panic of my heartbeat. I can't breathe. Heavy pressure compresses my abdomen, forcing some of the air I'd gulped in before impact away.

And I lose Aric's hold.

He reaches for me as the sea swallows him, drawing him down much faster than it takes me. In a blink and a terrified, watery scream, he's gone.

I flail, my hands slicing through the water trying to find him even though I know he's not there. A cry vibrates through my chest, costing me a little more air.

The glimmering light of the surface fades as I'm sucked down. Instead of becoming buoyant, my body sinks toward the bottom of the ocean like a lead weight.

But something's wrong. Aric went straight through the gate or the portal or whatever barrier separates the realms.

But me? I'm still just floating here.

Alone. Alone. Alone.

Desolation is a feeling as dark as the depths that grow thicker all around me.

The shadows descend, and through the current, a large shark swims past with a powerful flick of its fin. A million fish ascend from the darkness to twirl around me, each dark body glinting with sharp silver scales that cut everywhere they brush against my flesh. Beady little eyes track me as I spin around, containing the scream that wants to steal the dwindling air remaining in my lungs.

Something cold and slimy slithers along my calf and wraps around my shin, tentacles suctioning to my body as it tightens like an anaconda squeezing its prey. Air bubbles containing the rest of my ration of oxygen flit to the surface along with the remainder of my hope.

The beast below me lets out a menacing, rumbling bellow, and my leg aches as it's jerked down. Everything hurts. It feels like I'm being ripped apart, the burning in my lungs is simply the cherry on top of the torture sundae.

I wiggle and kick and bend to claw the monster off of me. Salt stings my eyes, but I catch a glimpse of a beastly creature.

Rough barnacle textures an enormous face that's much too humanlike in appearance. A thick brow lines his features, but I can't fully make out his eerie features. Spikes line the upper part of its many arms that reach out for me. Six rows of sharp teeth glint inside the open maw of the kraken that's prepared to eat me like a snack.

Each tug brings me closer to my death.

Crimson blood floats like ink as I bleed into the sea. I lose my shit as I kick repeatedly at the tentacle holding me hostage.

No. Nope. I'm not going down like this.

My wolf lends me strength, and the next hit loosens the kraken's hold enough that I gain back an inch, then two.

Rushing water is a distraction I can't afford, but I turn anyway. Then duck the fuck out of the way as the shark angles his body, zooming through the water right for me.

Son of a bitch!

The tentacle latches onto me tighter than Spanx after a Thanksgiving meal, cutting off my blood supply like a tourniquet.

Slowly, so I can really see my death coming, the kraken pulls me toward its mouth.

My shoes just scrape along the first row of teeth when a pair of large hands clench around me. I fight against the sudden terrifying hold, but then I'm pulled up through the thick water.

I glance back to see Torben looking like some furious sea god. His long locks drift in the darkening sea. He's beautiful.

And fucking terrifying when he's furious.

Back and forth I'm wrenched like a tug-of-war pull toy until Torben thrusts out a hand just above my head. Magic twirls like a current. His fire dies on impact, but the water warms and warms until it's sweltering, morphing the cold ocean around us into a bubbling hot tub. Light burns brightly inside Torben, turning him into a glow stick of hellfire that becomes a beam driving the creatures who live in the dark away from us. Screeching loudly, the tentacle loosens and then releases, leaving behind a wicked bruise.

That same power that lives inside me flares with gratitude as I turn in Torben's arms and wrap my own around his narrow waist.

He seems shocked, suspended in the heated

current as his magic subsides. Tentatively, his arms close around me in a hug that would be far more enjoyable if I could breathe in the scent of him… or breathe at all.

But I still feel protected in his strong arms.

His fingers trail up my back, tickle along my neck, and skim along my jaw until he's cupping my face. Sea green eyes close slowly and a shiver races through my entire body as he comes closer. Bringing his mouth to mine, he covers my lips in a soft caress that grows steadily harder. His lips are softer than I expected, and so warm against the cold chill of mine. Torben forces them apart and breathes life into me.

I don't understand how, but it fills my lungs and eases my anxious pulse.

It's a small breath, but enough to keep me from passing out just yet. My heart tightens when he pulls away, leaving me shocked and bewildered that he cares enough to keep me alive.

It wasn't a kiss. It wasn't intimacy. It was just… magical air shared between a girl and fucking Aquaman.

Not a big deal at all.

For a man who fears nothing, there's a healthy dose of apprehension in his expression when he pulls away, but it clears in an instant, making me question whether it had ever been there at all.

Mossy green eyes so dark they're nearly black tell me all I need to know.

Hang the fuck on…

I cling to him as his powerful arms propel us downward. The ocean fights us, trying to claim Torben while rejecting me altogether, but he's not leaving me behind.

I don't have time to dwell on whether or not that's a good thing. After experiencing the ocean from hell, what waits for me on the other side is a mystery I'm not sure I want to uncover.

But fuck it. I'm out of options, and I'm out of time.

Torben's air is bleeding slowly from my lungs as black dots start to pepper my vision.

He struggles and kicks and swims against the tide, a force of nature in the body of a hellish god.

I'm on the verge of passing out when the sea finally yields. It claims me.

The current sweeps us up in a rollercoaster ride that makes me nauseous. Dips and curves make my stomach drop through my feet until we enter a swirling whirlpool, then it leaves me altogether.

Through it all, Torben doesn't release me. One hand is a bar against my back, his fingers digging into my shoulder while the other crosses my back with his hand on my ass.

Wrapping my legs around him, I hold on, burying my face in his neck. I whimper as we swirl faster and faster until the bottom drops out.

I'm falling once again, this time headed straight for Hell itself.

Chapter Eighteen

The Realm of Hell

Rhys

Magic tears at my skin, threatening to rip away at the flesh. Then it stops. Only dry wind slides over every inch of my body, and then a hard impact slams through me. My head jars against Torben's hard chest as he takes the brunt of the impact. My body whips back as the force knocks me off of his protecting body and into the dirt, hard enough to rattle my teeth. My fingers dig into dry, coarse strands as I come to a careening stop.

Grass.

White, dead grass sprouts around me, but a strange rush of water still roars in my ears.

I peer up to the intensity of the sound, only to find it isn't water at all. It's fire. A wide stream of lapping flames rushes only inches away from where my arm lies on a riverbank.

Two inches to be exact. I landed two inches away from a fiery death.

The heat of it sears over me, stealing away my breath and drying away the icy water that clings to my clothing and hair.

I roll away from the bizarre river and stare up at the crimson colored sky above.

"These realms are going to kill me." I exhale defeatedly as my wolf surges to heal my numerous cuts and bruises.

"Well, they are meant for the dead," Latham says logically from where he casually reclines against a boulder.

"Not far now." Torben stands steadily, as if he didn't just leap from a mountaintop, save my sorry ass, kiss me for totally logical reasons, then hit the ground like some kind of Great-Value brand god of thunder. He brushes off his drying jeans, and I realize he doesn't have a single rugged hair out of place. His beard is immaculate, and I'm starting to question if beard magic is his real hidden talent.

"What are you looking at?" he asks gruffly when he catches me staring at how the firelight glints off of his perfectly coiffed strands of facial hair. It's like the gods themselves blessed his face.

Don't say his beard. Don't say his beard. Don't say—

"Your beard is so pretty," I say before I can think better of it.

A line creases his brow, and a snicker of laughter

shakes through Aric. Latham's quiet smile shines in his eyes. Torben gives me nothing more than a grunt.

"I think the lack of oxygen has fucked with your head," Torben grumbles like he didn't just try to save me with his kiss of life. "If there are no more compliments you have to get off your chest, we'll keep moving," Torben finally tells me, barely giving time to breathe before forcing us onward.

I swallow hard and try not to roll my eyes at him as well as my own stupidity.

Latham offers me his hand, and I slide my fingers against his palm as he lifts me to my feet. Aric peers around at the open expanse of dry grassy plains.

"Home sweet home," the dragon shifter says quietly.

At the sound of Aric's deep timbre, a meow rumbles out of the bag in his hand and pure fire leaps right out. In a blaze, my small house cat shifts into enormous translucent flames that sketch his delicate features against the landscape.

I blink at Loki. He purrs happily as he soaks in the heat of this hellish realm.

"This is Hell?" I look up at Aric as we trail after Torben's enormous steps.

"This is the entrance to Helheim, technically. It'll lead us to what's more commonly thought of as Hell." Latham picks something from my hair before flicking a soggy strand of seaweed to the ground.

I try to find some normalcy in what we're doing. I'm on a journey into Hell. That should be unsettling.

"Think of it like the suburbs." Aric smirks, clearly having picked up on my aversion to the 'burbs.

It settles in a scurry of nerves under my skin that I'm now officially in Hell. Okay… Hell adjacent.

Worst of all, my mother has been here for years.

"My mother, is she dead?" I ask quietly, my stomach dipping at the thought of it.

Latham tilts his head to look at me from the corner of his eye.

"No. The inhabitants of these realms are one of several things—newcomers, those who pass on to the afterlife, gods like Torben, creatures born here like Aric, or the offspring of gods, like myself."

"What category does my mother fall into?" And what category do I fall into for that matter?

Latham shakes his head, his inky locks fanning across his eyes as he scans our surroundings.

"I don't know. I'd never met your mother until the day I left here with orders to retrieve you."

It occurs to me then that Latham is the informed one of the bunch. And even he isn't well informed about me…

What kind of twisted secrets was my mother hiding?

A wave of heat washes through the air, and I barely collide into Aric to avoid the splashing of the river. The breath in my lungs shudders, and I try hard to focus on the information I've just been given.

My mother is an inhabitant of Hell. Possibly a goddess, more likely a creature. A reckless wolf like

me perhaps…

"If Torben is a god, why is he in Hell?"

Aric chuckles as he wipes a hand down his face to stop the sweat that's beading against his forehead.

"It's not like the fairy tales of gods or goddesses that you're familiar with." Aric slides his attention to me, and his humor seems distracted as his gaze travels from my eyes to my lips… to the sweat soaked shirt that's now clinging to my breasts. "Gods aren't always good. Even the good ones aren't very good," he whispers with a shake of his head. "The bad guys don't walk around with pitchforks and pointed tails. Hell is ruled by gods, and just like in real life, it's impossible to see which ones are the good guys and which ones are the bad."

That information is a bit harder to process. Because it means my mother might belong in Hell for a reason. She might be evil…

But Latham's from Hell and he isn't evil.

And Aric… well… maybe I should just stick to the example of Latham for now.

A single deserted tree stands tall up ahead. It's the first one I've seen, and it splays out against the red horizon like a skeleton greeting us with open arms. Not a single leaf adorns the white limbs that line the trunk like the shattered lines of a cracked window. It feels ominous in a simplistic way.

It's just a tree.

Nothing more.

A cawing strikes through the quiet and I leap at

the sound of it. My shoulder jostles into Latham's, and his warm hand instantly covers mine.

"It's just a hell hawk," he tells me.

I squint at the blushing sky to see a creature resting on the lowest bony limb of the tree. Its inky feathers are sleek and natural, but the blood-red eyes looking back at me are not.

It's just a hell hawk. Totally normal.

I can't even make eye contact with the thing.

We carry on, following the path of the riverside, but it unnerves me to walk beneath the clawing branches of the dead tree. Those hellacious eyes burn against my face as I walk as casually as possible beneath the creature.

"Hate birds," Aric murmurs.

"I thought dragons hated mice." Latham looks up at the demonic thing, and he's the only one who has the balls to make eye contact.

"Dragons hate all the darting little beasts. Too fast to track and nefarious as hell. Fucking monsters is what they are." He shakes his head hard, and I note how much he's slumped down at his shoulders as we slip under the watchful red eyes following us.

A loud squawking shrieks out at us. It sounds like the sky is falling and a hailstorm of satanic birds are raining down on us. Aric snatches my hand in his and drags me away. His boot catches on a twisting tree root. He staggers and takes me down with him, and we land in a cloud of dust with my legs sprawled between his. My fingers dig into his shirt as he sits up,

lifting me against him to see the destruction that must have happened.

Except… only uncontrollable laughter echoes in the wake of the chaos.

Latham still stands just a foot away from the bird. His smile is so broad a sweet dimple peeks out against his cheek as an unfiltered chuckle rumbles out of him while we lay sprawled in a tangle of limbs in the dirt.

A big hand wraps around mine, and I'm once again being rescued by the scowling face of a sexy giant.

Torben pulls me away from Aric and nods for me to walk forward.

"Come on," he tells me. "I'll protect you from the scary sounds of nature from here on out."

A smile tilts my lips, and I walk away in sync with Torben's quick, enormous steps.

"The damn thing was going to peck our eyes out!" Aric hollers after his friend, but Torben just rolls his eyes as he keeps going. "Would have vomited them back up and fed them to her demon bird babies too," Aric adds, and at that, the smallest smirk pulls at the corner of Torben's full lips.

My heart startles awake at the hint of amusement that's shining in the serious man's mossy green eyes. His personality mirrors his eyes so well—he's jaded.

And I bet he'll never tell a living soul why. Or maybe he's just like me and he doesn't understand why himself.

Sometimes our life isn't what we make it, but what

others choose to make it.

Like my mother.

And like the gods who cast this beautiful warrior of a man into the bowels of Hell.

Perhaps we're the same.

Hours fall away like that without a hint at the time. No sun dares to cross the bleeding red sky. It never fades lighter or darker. It simply burns us harder with each passing second that fades away into the nothingness of the desert.

"The bridge will be just up the bend here," Torben says suddenly.

I glance up at the unending sloshing of the river. It's straight as a beam. The length of it carries out into the distance like an artist's study on perspective.

My nose scrunches with a painful reminder of the burn against my flesh as I look from the unbending river to the man at my side.

"Bend?" I ask, and my throat stings from the hoarseness of my voice.

He glances down at me. His attention alone reminds me of the press of his lips against mine.

Heat rushes to my already warm face as I look away.

"The bend." He waves a big hand in front of him as if it's obvious.

I look up at the fiery stream once more.

It's literally as straight as Mary's not-so-secret dating profile on wolves seeking wolves dot com. Not even a hint of a curious drifting slant, I'm telling you.

176

"Squint your eyes," Torben commands.

Painful lines crinkle around my eyes as I search out this nonexistent bend in the riverside.

Nothing. Not even a rock along the bank can be seen to curve the trail of flaming water.

"Use your other sight," Torben encourages, and it slowly sinks in.

"You mean my wolf's?" My eyebrows lift as I meet his gaze.

He nods.

My eyes narrow.

"How would you know how to use my *other* sight?" My head tilts and he swiftly looks away into the vast nothingness. "What are you, Torben?" I ask quietly.

"A warrior. Powerful enough to lead many ventures into many realms, and most importantly, powerful enough see the bend up ahead. And to tell you to mind your pretty fucking business." His jaw clenches, and he doesn't even look my way as he strides ahead with even faster steps.

He leaves me, but also stays close. The space he clings to between him and me is very obvious.

He's an asshole. Clearly. But he's an attentive asshole.

So that's something.

I shake my head at his bitter temperament and exhale the heavy sigh that's clouding my lungs. My attention lifts to the fiery point in the distance where the red river kisses the crimson sky. My wolf hums to life within me, warming me to impossible temperatures as magic flares like a single sparkler at the center of my chest.

My eyes focus and unfocus. Then, a shift in sight comes together, heightening my vision, my hearing, my sense of smell, and all my senses.

And there it is. The river sways up ahead, drifting hard to the right where it rushes down faster and faster to an abrupt edge.

"A firefall." A surprised breath of air escapes in a gasp.

Torben stops in his tracks with a wave of dust billowing around his hard warrior's body. The corner of his lip twitches as his eyes shine brightly into mine.

"Just past the bend," he adds to my statement.

I smile like I finally passed the shifter exam on the third try.

Pride blooms in my chest but the encouraging smile doesn't linger on his hardened features.

"Keep moving," he grumbles.

All the achievement in me rips away.

And I keep fucking moving.

***

My dawdling steps pick up the pace when that damn bend finally leads the four of us to the right. I even pass Torben in my excitement to see the bridge that leads us to the entrance of Hell.

"Slow down, princess," he hisses.

"Slow down?" I turn to look back at the three men

watching me with big, awestruck attention. "You've done nothing but bark at me to speed up this entire time!"

"Keep your voice down!" Torben warns on a hushed growl.

Latham's brow lowers, and I've never seen him so serious before.

Then he's running, his steps blaze over the ground with fire catching at his feet. Aric rushes forward as well, his eyes suddenly burning brighter than the sky light. Torben's arm flexes as his fist lifts high, and I know he's about to use the magic deep inside himself.

I just don't understand why.

My boots stagger, and I come to full stop.

"Okay," I whisper. "I'll slow down. Calm your god complex already." I lift my hands to placate the warrior and the two men who are now passing him in a blur of hellfire.

My heart pounds as a growl shakes through my chest. My wolf snorts with aggression. I can't breathe. Something bad is near. I can feel it.

Sense it.

I look up toward Latham, but the beautiful, tormented man is no longer there. A wolf of flaming hellfire rips from his flesh. It lands on four giant paws that eat up the dry land, its claws slashing into the ground with every running step it takes. A vengeful growl parts its mouth with sparking fire roaring up its throat.

Fenrir.

Chapter Nineteen

The Guardians of Hell

Rhys

My wolf doesn't question life. She doesn't pause or consider the outcome.

She just fucking reacts.

She wreaks chaotic magic through my veins as her strength alone sends a shriek of pain tearing from my lips. Her snapping teeth come first. A cracking of bone and a sizzling of magic is all I remember before my body is her own. She consumes me, snarling and snapping her jaws as she turns and races in perfect rhythm with the hellhound now at my side. Bright starry eyes peer over at me for a single second, burning more brightly than the flaming fur of his fenrir, and then we're attacking.

A beast of a man towers above us. He's four times

Torben's size, a literal fucking giant. His bulky arm is as big as a tree and grasps a flaming branch like a weapon that arcs downward, aiming to smash us into the ashy dirt beneath my paws. I jump over his strike lithely, my wolf not only strong but graceful. Fire singes my tail, but my wolf is already taking aim. Sharp teeth rip into thick flesh. My jaws sink harder into the giant's leg.

The putrid taste of his black blood fills my mouth, but I don't yield.

Loki's mewl is low and vicious as he races up and slashes at the beast with ferociously sharp claws. No longer my little ball of grey fur, his hellcat form is huge and glowing with the fires of Hell as he attacks, trying to protect me by eradicating the threat.

A blur of fire rushes past us, climbing higher, and then Latham's fenrir catches the meaty wrist of our attacker. Growls and roars shake through the air, but it's the abrupt earthquake below that sends me flailing to the ground with a hard kick from the giant's bare foot.

Dirt billows around me as I hit the ground hard.

"No pass!" the enormous man booms.

Spitting fire laps up from the cracked soil. Torben stands several yards away, and once more he raises his powerful fist. It comes down like a lash of lightning, fire blazing out like an explosion of glass shattering on concrete. The warrior's eyes blaze just as hot, searing with magic as he assesses the giant with cruel violence in his gaze.

Sparking embers surround me. The rushing river

is just behind the giant and the steel metal bridge can narrowly be seen between his trunk-like legs. The heat of hellish magic burns through the air. It's all I see, all I smell, all I feel.

Until a thrashing wind suddenly pushes down on me. A scathing sound of total destruction roars through it all, and my wolf halts in her tracks at the beastly growl hissing down from the crimson skies.

A pure black dragon with glowing symbols and lines etching all across its lengthy torso rises up. Its wide wings and even the tip of its flaming tail soars over me. It swoops down and the giant staggers, shaking the land when he crashes down on his ass with the force of an earthquake. The shadow of the creature alone envelops the giant, and it too looks up with wide, fearful eyes.

And that's when I take my shot.

Dirt flicks into my narrowed eyes. Fire licks at my paws as I leap over the clawing flames reaching up from the shattered land. But not even the burn of a thousand embers would stop me now.

My claws sink deep before I shove off hard. The wind catches at my limbs as total weightlessness sinks in. A dragon's talon crashes down atop the chest of the giant just as I extend my body and sink my canines into the leathery skin at the base of his neck. A strange magic warms deep inside of me and my growl emits deeper, a painful breath burning up my throat. Magic as scorching as the blaze of the sun stings from my tongue and sizzles across the giant's throat and face.

We've pinned him.

I can taste his screams that linger like ash clinging to the air.

His arms flail above me, batting at the dragon's massive talons slicing up his face. Hands fumble against the dirt.

And then flames fly overhead like a white flag meant to kill his enemies. The fiery branch the giant wields swipes down on Aric, and despite my wolf's determination, I release my hold and watch my friend free-fall like a battered bird fumbling to the ground. I tumble down but land on readied feet. The dragon's roar is enraged as it huffs out smoke and carefully restrained fire.

I move away, my paws treading backward from the giant as the dragon strides closer and closer with the flames of Hell held just at the back of his throat. The giant mumbles something as he kicks Latham's hellhound off for the third time and flings Loki away like my enormous cat is a mere annoyance rather than a true threat.

Latham stands, morphing with ease into his human form. On waning steps he comes slowly forward, his blood pooling across this ashy ground. The giant beast rears back the fist that clutches the fiery branch, and stares Aric dead in the eye.

Then he throws it with the force of a hundred men.

It launches through the air like an arrow aimed perfectly at its target. It's quicker than the wind, barely visible to the naked eye, and there's not enough time for Aric to react.

A blaze of familiar fiery magic flickers in the air, and not a hound or even a beast catches the flaming branch.

Smoke wafts around Latham's body as he appears from the ether. Using his impenetrable strength, he rips the branch from the air in a collision of cracking wood. He holds the enormous branch in one hand, his gaze unflinching as he looks the monstrous giant in the eye.

Latham's fingers tighten, his knuckles turn white, and the wood splinters in his fist as he cracks it into two solid pieces. The broken branch lands with a loud thud upon impact as Latham drops the weapon like it's a puny stick to be forgotten.

"My club!" The giant's face twists in anger. A war scream booms across the dry lands in sound waves full of agony. Thunderous magic shakes all around me at the sound of his rage. The trembling power raises the hackles of my fur. It sways the godly splintered cracks of fiery ground.

Pain strikes deep into my sensitive ears and my wolf whines as she lowers her head in an attempt to protect herself. It seeps into her so deeply, prickling fear strikes at the hidden well of her magic, weakening her. It's something I've never felt from the reckless wolf in my entire life.

She has always been the strong one.

Always.

Anger soars through me, and I shift in the blink of an eye. The heated air is a caress against my bare skin that mimics the warmth I blanket over my wolf,

locking her safely away in the center of my chest, shielding that sweet bond I have with my protective wolf who has saved me time and time again in my life.

It's my turn to save her.

A slick trickle slips down my ear and along my neck, but the noise of the giant is nothing more than a stabbing numbness that sinks all the way through my skull.

The others look like my wolf felt.

Loki screeches with a pain filled cry as the hellcat scrambles back. Latham is curled on the ground with his hands tightly over his ears. The fierce dragon has it's flaming tail curled around his friend, but the misery on the creature's face is clear as it roars and flinches with each new wave of magical pain that's sent out to them.

And Torben. Torben is crawling on his knees. Blood covers his neck and chest, but he relentlessly crawls through the flames to the monster attacking us with little effort.

With all my waning strength, I run.

My feet rush over the quaking ground. In a blur of speed, I run past the giant, leap over the lines dividing the ground, and skid to a stop right in front of the two shifters who need me most right now.

My heart soars, and with a sweep of my hand, I pick up the one thing that seems important to our attacker.

That fucking broken stick.

"Hey!" I scream. "Hey, ogre!" I shake the

battered, fiery branch at him.

The shaking stops.

"Me giant!" he roars in correction, though I can barely make out his words over the ringing in my ears.

"Yeah?" I walk casually across the dry land. Everything is numb, and even my balance feels off without the sound of the rushing fire in the swift moving river as I stride closer to it. The tips of my toes stop just an inch from the edge of the cliff, just near the descent of licking flames and molten fire.

I look up at the confusion in the giant's eyes. My hands lift high, and his gaze follows that motion.

"Go fetch, ogre." And then I release his beloved branch over the fiery falls.

That painful roar of magic rips from his lips once more, and I fall to my knees with the slicing pain bleeding from my ears. Urgent footfalls shake the ground even stronger. My hands fumble against the dirt as I'm swayed toward the edge of the cliff.

The giant leaps right over me. His shadow is the last I see of him as he chases after his precious weapon. His slicing screams carry on though, crashing waves of magic all through the hot air.

The land shakes from the sounds of his misery. The ground splits open even more. There is no up or down. Everything teeters.

The last thing I see is a widening flash of blue eyes.

And then I fall too.

Chapter Twenty

A Hard Night

Rhys

Hot wind rips at my hair. The world is a haze of many shades of red, but I can't open my eyes to any of it. My senses are numb and battered. My body isn't much better.

I tense all over.

And wait for impact.

The slamming collision comes from above instead. A man drops from the sky and strong arms wrap all around me. My lashes lift just slightly, and Torben's bloodied face is the first thing I see. His beard whips in the wind just as much as his long hair. His gaze never once looks my way.

He's entirely focused on what lies below.

Something I nearly forgot. Until it jars into us. My head knocks against his as his boots hit the ground with a cloud of dust and dirt washing up over us. It clings to his hair and settles against my flesh as he straightens from his superhero landing.

His deep green eyes shift over my face. He traces my wide eyes, the curve of my cheek, and finally my lips. An inch of space separates me from the Viking of a man. The ripples of his muscles show beneath a drenched and dirty shirt.

He truly is a hero. He never once gave up, even after it was too late for me.

And now he's saved me twice... Three times... Wow, I really should mumble a thank you now and then, I guess.

Something about that thought quivers inside of me and I lean into him even more, our breaths meeting just before our lips.

But our lips never touch.

Because his mouth opens with a stream of words....

That I can't hear.

"What?" I ask as loudly as I can, but my own voice sounds far off in the distance.

His lips move once more without sound.

"What?"

He flinches at the apparent sound of my words, so I try again.

"I can't hear you!"

He shakes his head hard and drops me to the

ground, my feet stumbling slightly. His now free hands shove through his messy blond locks.

Fuck. I can make out that word. I watch his lips intently to try to understand more.

Fuck—fuck—fucking woman.

"Excuse me!" My hands hit my nude hips and his attention follows the motion, making me suddenly aware of how very naked I am right now. Again.

Doesn't matter.

"Don't curse me. I'm right here. You're being rude!" I glare at the man who just rescued me.

He turns on me with a deadly stare like a total caveman about to drag me off to be claimed.

I don't know why my hips shift at the idea of that.

It's just his stature. He's big in that natural way that makes you want to climb him. Makes you want to see how small he can make you feel as he pins you beneath him. Makes you want to lower yourself over him and find out if every inch of him is just as proportionate…

"I said this fucking woman is going to get me in trouble!" he roars, and his gravelly growl suddenly sinks in.

My mouth falls open, and I listen intently.

The sound of a beautiful hellacious waterfall can be heard. If I close my eyes, I can imagine it to be just that instead of falling flames of fire.

In the distance, I hear the thudding footsteps of the retreating giant as he disappears from sight, cradling his precious broken branch.

My hearing is healed.

The part of me that's never really been mine but my wolf's is now one. I'm her and she is me. We share the same healing magic. The same emotions. The same beautiful soul.

Dampness stings my eyes as I look up at Torben with a sudden smile.

"I'm a wolf," I say through the excited, tender emotions filling me.

Narrowed eyes look at me like I'm fucking crazy.

"Fucking woman," he whispers to himself as he walks off into the copse of thinning trees.

A flicker of a blaze hits the air just before Latham walks right out of nothing at all. His wild gaze searches me, his hands trembling against my tangled hair.

"You're alright?" He lifts my hands then turns my head this way and that, pausing on the dry blood along my throat.

"I'm fine," I whisper and swallow down the epiphany I've just had.

A smile still pulls at my lips, and I might never get over the fact that I feel like my best friend has finally come home to me.

It's a strange, empowering sensation.

Wind presses downward, fanning the flames of the river before an enormous dragon touches down at my side. Thick legs are eye level with me, while his chest and body are well over two stories tall. Inky scales glint against the firelight. A swaying tail sweeps forward, and the torch at the end of it swooshes past

me as the length of it curls around my hips, bringing me closer in small, inching steps. He drags me right up to him, his head lowering before dark, sliced pupils fixate on me. My own features shine in his beautiful, monstrous eyes. I lift a hand and ever so lightly run my fingertips over his chest. The ridges of his scales are like smooth leather. A beautiful armor.

Laughter hums from my lips.

"You're the kind of beast who would hoard a girl like me away if this were a fairy tale," I whisper quietly.

Scales shimmer brighter, and magic crackles with the scent of smoke blooming around us. His shift happens all at once, and Aric's smooth arms wrap around me where his tail once was. But a part of his creature is still present. Large black wings take their time sinking into the flesh of his back as my hand drifts higher, sliding over the leathery feel of them before they disappear entirely. Soft skin is all that's left, my fingers still skimming there lightly.

"Careful," Aric warns, his words spoken so close I can feel them against my tongue. "I still might hoard you away and keep you for myself, Love."

My heart free-falls harder than when I fell from a cliff just seconds ago. How does he do that? How has no one in my entire life ever made me feel the way this crazy killer of a man does?

The noise of someone clearing their throat rather roughly jars me, and I realize how lost I was in his fire-kissed eyes. I tear my attention away and clothing is shoved right in my face.

"How about we put a nice, safe layer of clothing

on?" Latham offers me a shirt and a pair of jeans before shoving another round of clothing toward his friend.

It's then that I realize how very on display I am.

Latham's gaze dips low, but he looks away toward the sparse tree line.

When I glance back up to Aric though…

Ravenous hunger consumes his eyes, and that rawness trails down the length of my body before slowly meeting my gaze.

"I think we should clean up first," Aric rumbles, his hot breath fanning across my collarbone.

Latham still doesn't look at us, but he nods as he points toward the land where Torben is collecting full size trunks of trees over his shoulder like they're just a bit of firewood.

"Should make camp," Torben grumbles.

"There's a sprite's cove deep in the forest here," Latham says as if he didn't hear his grumpy friend.

"Should rest up before heading further," Torben adds but is speaking to literally no one at this point.

My eyes narrow on the ash white trees Latham just called a forest.

"Sprite's cove? As in a cove of water?" I ask, also ignoring Torben's grumbles. If I'm prioritizing needs, getting clean beats shelter at this point.

Latham smirks at that question, but before he answers he disappears altogether. The fire barely has time to fizzle out before he's back, holding my small grey cat who has now returned to normal. Including

the unimpressed scowl on his little adorable face. He puts him down, and Loki shakes out his fur before trotting off to explore, fully content that I'm fine for now.

Even my cat's a psycho now. Is this what Hell does to people?

Latham leads us after him, motioning toward the cover of trees.

"This place has been a dry wasteland since the beginning of time. Then the dark elves came, other forest creatures followed. Water nymphs and sprites. Trees grew as their magic spread here and there where it could. It drove Hela mad to see life blossoming so close to her home." The soft tone and the smile that brightens Latham's sharp features chases out the torment that always hides behind his eyes.

"Are sprites like pixies then?" I follow with my clothes bunched in my hands as Latham guides us past the thin, tall tree trunks.

Laughter rumbles out of Aric in a way that warms my chest.

"Not one fucking bit," he says. "Pixies are annoyingly helpful bursts of happiness. Sprites are fucking evil."

I look at him with wide eyes. A very obvious question falls from my lips.

"Then why are we going there?" Haven't I been through enough for one day?

"They're too small to attack. They're flighty around anything larger than themselves." Latham slips through a pair of trees, and the space around us is growing tighter by the second. Thousands of gray and white bark trees are everywhere, growing so closely together it's hard to slip through. The forest scrapes at my thighs and back as I follow after him.

"They'll fuck with you. But never to your face," Aric adds.

"I don't know how much farther I can go—" Another trunk drags roughly over my ass as I try to squeeze through a space Latham's lithe body just disappeared into. I stagger out the other side and my mouth falls open the moment I get through.

Light patches of pale green grass carpet the ground that shimmers with sand and rock. The pebbles are a rainbow of color. Amber pinks, mint greens, deep jades, pale lavender, ruby reds, and so many more line the shore of a glinting sapphire cove.

"Oh my gods," I whisper as the magic settles into my very soul.

A warm hand settles low against my back as Aric's smooth chest skims against mine, teasing my nipples lightly. "Wait until you feel it," he tells me, and a different kind of magic coils low in my stomach.

I swallow hard and try not to regard him or his sensual words.

"We can use this?" I ask cautiously while I take a safe step back from the sexy shifter to place my clothes down hesitantly over the beautiful smooth pebbles.

Latham nods, his starry eyes catching the shimmering magic in the depths of his eyes as he takes

it all in. But he doesn't come closer.

He leans against a tree instead. A calmness blankets over us here, and I understand that look in his features.

It's peace.

No one is taunting me here. No one hates me here. No one's chasing me or wants me dead.

It's like Heaven snuck into Hell.

I'll stay here in this nirvana for as long as they let me.

A roaring yell and thunderous feet trample over my tranquility, and I'm alert in a single second. I turn on my bare feet.

Just in time to be splashed in the fucking face by Aric's cannon ball dive into the cove. Water streams down my cheeks when I glare at his head that bobs up from the beautiful, gleaming surface.

"Get in!" he yells with no concern for the little squeaks of noise I hear hiding in the shadows around us. A quick flutter of wings and a scurry of mouse-like words pass around the circular open expanse we stand in.

But I suppose Aric's right, they haven't attacked us.

Yet…

I turn and look over my shoulder at Latham, the true voice of reason between the two shifters. His soft smile still ghosts his lips as he nods to me. "It's nice, like a sauna."

His attention slides down my back and even lower

before I turn away from him. Nudity has never been a self-conscious way of life in my pack. It's natural for the most part.

Then why does it feel so tense with sexual need even when I'm dressed for winter in the mountains around these men?

Warm pebbles caress my feet with each step I take. They're heated from the land and soft against my skin. My toes dip into the pure blue water. The unnatural cove ripples out from my disturbance. The temperature is like a hot bath, and I eagerly wade out into it.

Aric's attention never leaves me. His stare is just as warm as the water and sends tingles across my flesh, much like the magic glinting in the depths I'm sinking into. My nipples tighten as I hold his gaze, and I'm all too aware of the shifting of my thighs. An uneven breath pulls into my lungs. It all becomes too much.

I lower down as far as I can go and let the heat of the cove surround me as my head lowers fully under. My heart still taps incessantly against my ribs to stride through this beautiful water, swim right up to that intoxicating man, and do all the things I've wanted to do to him since the moment we met. Hiding below the surface, I calm my demanding thoughts as well as my lovesick heart.

As for my frustrated monster of a sex drive... that's a loss. All women understand that we can't do anything to fix that. It'll rage on until I or someone else slays the beast.

I kick off from the luxurious sandy bottom and

rise up from the waters. Moisture clings to my lashes as I open my eyes.

And one hell of a sexy man is standing right in front of me.

That deadly dark smile of his parts his lips.

"Told you it'd feel good," he whispers like he's the god of deviance and desire.

Shit.

Heat burns my cheeks.

Is it too soon to sneak back under the water again?

Droplets trickle from his fingertips as he lifts his hand to my face. He skims his palm along my jawline, down my neck, across my collarbone.

"So much blood on such a pretty face," he says as he tenderly swipes away the remains of battle that still stain my skin.

He stands tall, the surface hitting inches above his belly button where it meets my body just over the curve of my breasts. I slink down to cover myself, feeling more intimate with Aric than I've ever felt with anyone in my entire life. Our reflections cast between us. Those images ripple away as he takes a single step closer. The slickness of his chest meets mine, my nipples tingling at the sensation of his body pressed perfectly against my own.

The warmth of his hand lingers along the side of my throat.

His head dips low and an ache forms deep inside me.

"Can I kiss you again?" he whispers like it pains

him not to.

My wanting gaze never leaves his.

But something inside me cracks beneath the perfection of this fairy-tale moment.

"No," I answer suddenly, and it truly does pain me as much as my voice trembles to say it.

His mouth opens as his hand slides away. With a single step he steals all that delicious desire he gave me just moments ago.

"Sorry," he murmurs, and suddenly the cocky dragon shifter can't meet my eyes. He can't seem to look at me.

"I—" I breathe through the tense pressure of confused want and fear swirling between my body, head, and heart.

"Maybe we should go," Latham calls out to us.

I turn and he's staring up at the sky, avoiding looking at me as much as his friend is.

"Darkness falls quickly out here," Latham adds.

"Yeah." Aric's tone is cutting and awkward.

With heavy steps that push at the waves of the water, he passes me. Water streams down his perfect body, licking at the tattoos along his arms and neck, cascading down the muscular globes of his ass and corded legs. Latham offers him a black towel and he presses his face into it. As the two men stand side by side, they appear as though they were made from the mystical magic that surrounds us. The hard lines of their bodies, the sharpness of their jaws, and even the stance that they hold themselves in is the epitome of enchantment.

I wade to the shore with quiet steps. Warm water slides down my flesh, but I don't take the towel Latham holds out to me. I stare at Aric's back. He refuses to turn around. There's no hostility in him, but he won't face me. It seems he's…

Embarrassed.

Oh my gods, the psychotic dragon shifter is embarrassed.

And he's also wrong.

"I didn't *not* want you to kiss me," I say quietly.

The towel he ruffles his shaggy tawny hair with stops abruptly. Tension lines his shoulders, yet he still doesn't turn to me.

"I wanted you to kiss me," I add.

Latham arches his brow and looks from Aric to me and then back again. The fenrir lowers the unused towel, shrugs quietly and magics it away with a flick of his wrist. He peers down at the dirt and blood that paints him, and with another wave of magic, he's sparkling and spotless, distracting me slightly with his flourishes of magic.

Aric's feet shift, and he turns casually around. A half smile tilts his lips, but it doesn't hold any of that manic happiness of his.

It's fake.

"You don't have to explain, Love. I'm not fragile. I can take rejection." He tosses his towel carelessly to the ground, and once more Latham glares at his friend and then me as he twists his hand and, with a spark of magic, he cleans up the disposed and forgotten towel.

"That's not what I meant though," I start, but Aric quickly cuts me off.

"It's not a big deal. It's fine. I'm fine. You're fine. Fuck, even Latham's fine. Right, Latham?"

"No, actually. I wish you two would stop fucking ignoring me during your lover's quarrels." Latham speaks with a calm stream of annoyance that never once hints at hostility. But yeah, he's as pissed as I might ever see him.

"It's not a lover's quarrel," Aric replies preposterously. "We're not lovers. And that's fine. Like I said. We're fine. More than fine."

"Would you shut the fuck up?" I scream, leaning up on my tippy toes to really drive my point home to my hard-headed dragon shifter. "Shut. Up."

Both men look at me with wide eyes and open mouths.

But finally, they say nothing.

Finally.

"I didn't want you to kiss me because this moment isn't real! It's a blip of beauty in my life that won't last. This beautiful fucking fae magic will fade away by nightfall, and we'll be back to fighting off Hell and bringing me to my mother in hopes that I find somewhere I belong." My voice cracks as I look from Aric's warm russet eyes to Latham's cool blue irises. "I don't belong with you. Either of you! I don't belong anywhere." The emotion is thick in my throat, and no matter how hard I swallow, the feelings won't go away.

Quiet flits of wings settle into the silence that follows my outburst. The sprites are really settling in for this soap opera it seems.

Shit. Why did I say any of that?

"Elf," Latham says in the quietest voice.

I blink at him in confusion.

"You said fae magic. It's not faerie magic, it's elfin magic. Much more powerful. Darker. Not the same." The more Latham explains, the more his voice dwindles off into nothingness. He just stares at me like that lost look in his eyes is finally sinking in and consuming him whole. "And you do belong. Especially with us," he whispers.

Aric prowls toward me. His confident steps eat up the space between us and he takes my hand slowly. He holds it and brings my palm up flat against his smooth chest. The strong drumming of his heart beats against my fingertips.

"I lied. You're not something I want to hoard away, Rhys." The way his deep rumbling voice says my name sends a shiver straight through me. "You don't fit in because you're not a piece of a common collection. You're rare." His hand tangles through my wet hair, his sweet words tangling deeper into my heart than he'll ever know. "Don't ever worry about fitting into a society of stones when you're a fucking diamond."

"Diamonds actually aren't rare," Latham murmurs, but his sound and constant logic is ignored as I lean in and slam my lips to Aric's.

His tongue parts my lips. Fingers tighten in my locks as he drags me hard against his body, my slick curves sliding against him in the best possible way. The friction is fluid, and the motion only reminds me of how badly I want to feel him sliding deep between my thighs.

My moan hums along his tongue, and his palm that's sliding down my hips lifts. A jerking sensation jars me against him before my back hits something behind me.

Aric pulls away just slightly as hooded eyes look from me… to something just behind me.

Warm and gentle hands slide around my waist, and I look over my shoulder to a sweet but hesitant smile.

Latham stands flush against my back, the water from my body seeping into his clothes as he stares down at me with parted but quiet lips.

They're always so careful with me. Protective. Kind.

Even like this, they don't pressure me.

And Latham's about to excuse himself.

I can tell in the way he takes a platonic step away from me, his hands still clinging to my curves despite how clear it is he thinks he should leave.

I arch backward in Aric's embrace, not fully turning to my fenrir but peering at him from over my shoulder. My arm lifts to slink my palm over Latham's neck before my fingers slide into his soft hair.

My lips hover over his as my eyes close slowly and I whisper, "Stay."

I never lean in. I don't make it easy for him. But I do hold my ground with my back to his chest. I let our breaths collide in an anxious battle of wants and wills that neither of us understand but both of us need. There's so much conflict in his eyes.

It's like he thinks he doesn't deserve even a second of happiness or pleasure.

But he's wrong.

And then his lips brush over mine.

His kiss is slow as he tastes me like he never wants this single moment to pass. Sharp nails dig into my hips where he holds me tightly against him. His tongue swirls over mine as another pair of warm lips press to my collarbone where Aric teases my flesh while Latham consumes my kiss. The two of them are this conflicting, caressing, biting mixture of total sexual desire.

Sharp teeth graze my nipple before sweeping over the peak with the flat of a sinful tongue. The dragon shifter has a rougher touch. Steady, gentle hands slide down the valley of my thighs, tracing ever so slowly over my body before stopping just above my clit. Latham's long fingers brush back and forth there, so close to where I need him, but not close enough.

My moan is a painful sound of want.

"Please," I beg between the press of his lips against mine.

A smile ghosts across his mouth with the next kiss, and his words rumble where his chest meets my spine. "Tell me you want me to fuck you with my hand," he demands, his tone hot and heavy with the warmth I'm used to but... his words shiver through me.

My lashes lift, and I look at the sweet man with the filthy mouth. My legs shift as those words circle around and around within my mind.

Aric drifts lower, his mouth leaving hot kisses all down my chest, my ribs, my stomach. Big hands hold my hips as he flicks his tongue over the sensitive skin along my upper thigh.

A haze clouds my thoughts with the two men taunting and teasing me, just inches from where I need them most.

"Tell Aric you want him to taste your sweet pussy," Latham whispers hotly along my neck. "Ask him to make you come against his mouth so he can lap up all your wetness before I slide into you hard and fast."

They're barely touching me, and I'm still panting from the thoughts drilling through my mind.

Aric nips at the skin just below my hip, and I buck in his hands, writhing against his tongue.

A hum of amusement rumbles through the dragon shifter's chest.

And still, no one touches me. No one sates that demanding feeling building with pressure between my thighs.

"Please," I whisper once more.

Latham presses another sweet kiss to my throat. "Please what?" he asks on a breathy wave across my flesh.

"Please make me come!" I grind out so quietly I

can't even think straight.

And then a wide, hot tongue parts my sex. It rolls over my clit hard and slow until I'm gasping in Latham's arms. He holds me against his chest and watches me curiously and intently while his friend fucks me with his mouth. I feel his gaze across the flush of my cheeks as he flicks his tongue over the lowest part of my neck, kissing and sucking and biting, all while watching me lose control of my every emotion.

Then he stops. Latham's breath is hot against my ear when he speaks next on a rumble of pure lust and sin.

"What are you thinking in that pretty mind of yours, Love?"

Reality shatters around me. My eyes fly open as two fingers sink deep yet gently into my slick sex. A ragged exhale escapes me like it's the first real breath I've ever tasted in my entire fucking life.

"I—I—I can't think," I blurt as Aric curves his fingers in a way that feels wrong but holy fucking dragon gods is it right. The cutting breath that enters my lungs is laced with a scream of wild pleasure that I've never felt before.

"Don't think." Latham hums along the curve of my neck, worshiping my body there with hot, open-mouthed kisses that tingle down like a current of magic is tongue-tied between his lips and Aric's. "Don't even speak if that feels better," he adds, but he doesn't touch me the way his friend does.

Latham's dirty mind is spilling out in explicit

words that make me wetter by the minute.

And yet he doesn't touch me any more than a few kisses, a few caresses of his hand…

Is he still hesitant?

It's then that I realize I want him to know exactly what I'm thinking.

I step back from Aric. Big blazing eyes stare up at me like a servant waiting for the next command. His hand lifts, and he pushes his palm casually across his wet lips, never once taking his gaze off of me. I take a moment to appraise the beautiful man still kneeling at my feet. His thighs are strong, corded with muscles that lead to lean hips. Swirling ink trails down his chest while hard lines veer even lower. His thick cock pulses against his lower stomach, and my eyes meet his just as an arrogant smirk tips the corner of his sexy lips. His sinful tongue rolls across his lower lip, and a shiver races right down my chest and through my clit.

I swallow dryly before turning ever so slowly to face the real problem we have here.

Latham's ocean blue eyes are like a stormfront brewing.

And all I want is lightning to strike.

Maybe even twice.

"You like to talk," I whisper, a smile etching my words.

Bashful amusement parts his lips as his own smirk melts my fucking heart on the spot.

Yet it's the sin that flashes in his pretty blue eyes that has me squirming.

"But you're not much of a doer, are you, Latham?"
My palms lift just as his eyebrows do at that statement.
Aric's laughter shakes through his chest as he runs his
fingers up and down the curve of my outer thighs.

My palms slide over Latham's jeans and along his
upper legs, trailing a teasing path… right to his waist.
A smooth button glides beneath my fingertips, and I
never once look away from that daring glint in his
gaze.

I know what I want. I want to make these men
never fucking forget me. I wish I could believe them.
I wish I could let my heart think that the three of us
will live a beautiful life in the midst of Hell.

But you can't imagine something you've never
had.

I have this moment though. I have them here and
now. And I want the memory of us to be an earth-
shattering bliss that haunts my mind every day of my
fucking life without them.

That single thought pushes me into action. My
fingers are steady when I unfasten the button, slide
down the zipper, and drop his jeans to the ground. He
stands in a black tee-shirt and a pair of boxers that
have a rather distracting bulge pressing hard against
them.

Anticipation thrums through me.

"You're a Hell god and yet you can't even make a
move on me, Latham." I tsk at him, and I can tell by
the playful straining smile on his face that I'm grating
on him just right.

Smooth, perfect lines guide my fingertips up his

hard stomach. I tug the hem of his shirt along with my exploring hands and pull it across his messy black hair and away. My gaze drops to the one thing left between us.

The flat of my palm pushes across the head of his cock just beneath the thin material of clothing. Thick lashes flutter, but he still stares me down.

"All talk and no play," I taunt, my fingers wrapping over the length of his shaft, sliding down the annoying fabric that separates me from what I want most.

A jagged breath shakes through his chest. His shoulders flex, and his Adam's apple works in his throat while his chin tilts up and he glares down at me with a shine of deadly intent in his violent blue eyes.

What. The. Fuck. Am. I. Doing?

I push a little more. A little more and a little more.

Because Latham is the lover. Not the fighter.

But I want both.

"Don't worry though," I whisper, leaning forward to tease my words along his neck just as he teased me. "Aric will make me feel good if you can't." Sadly, I drop my hand from his dick, his eyes blazing into mine as I take just one step back.

His entire body reacts the moment a single ounce of space separates us. His knees bend, his arms lower, and he grips me fully around my thighs before hauling me up against him like a fucking caveman taking what he wants.

His hand shoves between us, and the fabric

between us is pushed away. A smooth hardness slides over my wetness. My hands plant against his solid shoulders while my mouth gasps from the slick feel of him grinding back and forth along my folds.

Lashing lust burns in his eyes as he glares up at me, and his hold against my ass is just as claiming as his gaze.

"Don't ever fucking taunt me again, Love," he warns with a wicked smile that spreads into me.

But the moment a smirk kisses my lips, he sinks into me. Inch by inch he lowers me down, stretching me as far as I can go, and even then he thrusts to get deeper. A moan tears from my throat, raw and ragged.

From behind, warm lips kiss my shoulder while calloused hands continue to sweep up and down my curves. Shivers spread across my flesh with every caress of Aric's mouth against my neck. Longer fingers wrap ever so slowly around my throat. He digs in there to angle me just the way he needs to scrape his teeth across my neck.

Latham's hips move faster, his nails biting into the lowest part of my body, spreading me wider. The grip around my neck tightens as Latham's pace quickens. My screams turn to a gasp of sound as the air cuts past my lips. The stars behind my eyes are vivid within the void of darkness. Pleasure pulses with each breath that halts against my tongue. My lungs ache as much as the coiling bliss that's building with each passing second.

I need it. It's so close. I need *him*.

My nails claw at Latham's back as I bounce against him, thrusting myself harder down the thick length of his cock. His groan mirrors my gasping plea for more.

And more.

And more.

Until the stars burst open. The void burns out with color consuming the darkness. That unescapable tension snaps within me, and I scream out as the release pulses through me hard and fast.

From behind me, a growl of unfiltered dominance rumbles across my throat. The hold he has on me slips away and air swooshes into my burning lungs. My lashes flutter against the spots staining my vision. Everything feels heightened but blurred all at the same time.

It all slips away when my eyes meet Latham's.

There's a look of awe… or maybe lust… or maybe something else entirely that I see in Latham's features as he searches my face for every single sliver of pleasure he just gave me. He curiously takes it all in as his thrusts slow to really appreciate it.

To appreciate *me*…

Strong hands grip my waist. Aric's touch isn't soft and gentle as it was just moments ago. His hips are smooth along my ass as he melds against me. Latham pauses… but I don't know why.

Pressure pushes against my sex. My eyes widen as my walls clench against the two of them. Aric takes his time easing in, sliding along Latham while stretching me in such a way that I tremble in their arms. Jagged breaths groan over my shoulder. I feel the tension in his chest, the way he holds me, the way he forces

himself to go slow. My wetness is slick against their cocks, and neither of them want to rush me when all I want is to feel every fucking inch of them.

I lift myself ever so slowly, using Latham's shoulders as I go. Growls of pure pleasure rumble over my chest as well as my spine. A lost smile tilts my lips to hear their lust, so I do it again. I slide down faster against their thickness. Nails scratch deep across my flesh, stinging and tingling all through me.

"Fuck," Aric hisses, and so I do it harder. I slam down on them, leaning back into him to take as much as he can give.

His hand tightens on my hip while his other lifts over my shoulder. Long fingers shove harshly through Latham's hair as he drags him forward and their lips meet with a demanding collision. Aric puts all his frustration into the lashing of his tongue sliding against Latham's.

And Latham takes it. Even as Aric holds me in place and fucks us both. My head falls back on Aric's shoulder as he grinds against me as deep as he can go, putting delicious pressure in just the right places until I can't take it anymore.

My body quakes and my hands tremble against Latham, and the two of them hold me together as I completely fall apart in their arms. My screams silence nature. The flitting whispers of wings and words quiet instantaneously until only our groans of unleashed ecstasy are the only sounds.

Latham shifts and a final growling groan leaves his chest, he slams his lips to mine. He kisses me with a violent claim. He shows me after all this time he wants more than the innocent friendship he's always held between us.

He deserves so much more.

Aric's cock pulses deep inside my pussy as he stiffens behind me, his head leaning against my spine. His hot breath washes over me before a soft delicate press of his lips caresses my skin there. Latham pulls back just a fraction of an inch, his hair mixing with mine as our lips linger with quiet kisses passing the time.

The two of them wrap me up entirely, shielding me in their strength and affection. A sensation like I've never felt is wound tightly around me from every part of them that's tangled with every part of me.

It's a foreign and strange feeling for someone like me. It's never existed before. Not for me anyway.

It feels suspiciously like love…

Even if it's not.

Chapter Twenty-One

Ten Pack Abs

Torben

Rhys's hands plaster themselves against my abdomen as she clings to me. Her fingers are so small and lithe, I take a moment to marvel at how tiny she truly is. My own hands dwarf hers thanks to the giant blood running through my veins.

If I didn't know better, I'd think Rhys was fragile, but she's feisty and independent. When I was sent to retrieve her and bring her back to Hell, I didn't think she'd be so fucking strong. I expected a dainty flower, and while she looks the part, she doesn't act it.

Aric's leathery wings whip through the air, blowing Rhys's pale blonde hair around us. The strands caress my shoulder as the dragon lifts us off the ground with a single powerful pump. I'm surprised Aric has the strength to fly at all with what little sleep the four of us got. The darkness of nightfall only lasted about an hour.

Then the sky bled red once more.

And so our fucking journey continues.

"Holy fuck," she gasps from over my shoulder in the airy way she moaned for Latham and Aric as they pleasured her.

I stifle a groan and shift in my seat, hoping like hell Aric's dragon scales are thick enough that he can't tell how that simple little sound makes my dick hard.

My balls have been aching since I watched Rhys come from the shadows. The sight of her flushed skin and the way she parted her swollen, berry red lips is a vision I won't soon forget.

I hold it close and lock it away, knowing I'll need it when we get back to Hell.

The thought is a bucket of ice water against my libido. The tether of my duty is a noose around my neck, tightening each minute I spend in Rhys's presence.

I should throw the image of her writhing body straight into the fiery pits of Hell, because Rhys isn't my salvation. The small taste I've allowed myself to have of her was nothing but a thousand lashes of torment against my soul.

She'll never be mine, and I'll never be free enough to be hers.

Not that she wants me anyway. Not that I want

her.

So I'll stick with the fucking plan.

I'll stay away from her. I'll deliver her to Hela and reunite her with her mother.

And then I'll forget her.

Rhys's hands creep up my stomach, and then her fingers run along the dips and curves of my abs as she trails them back down.

My eyes squeeze closed, and I swallow as she tortures me beautifully.

Down. Down. Down.

A growl rumbles in my chest in a deep warning she doesn't heed. I cover both of her hands in one of mine before her fingers can brush along the hard, straining length of my cock.

My lashes open to the fiery sky, my gaze falling on Latham's figure as he stands between the two white horns on the dragon's head, his dark hair ruffles in the wind.

He's always so free when he's away from our homeland.

While I can't ever seem to mentally escape.

I try to keep that impenetrable reminder of who I am and where I belong at the front of my mind as her fingers slide deliciously against my body all over again. My nerves tingle until my flesh feels like it's humming for her.

A confusing comfort sets in. Her touch isn't a crawling sensation beneath my skin. She's the first person in centuries who actually feels good. I find myself wanting to hold her more and more. Just wrap myself up in her and let her scent soak into me.

I don't know if anyone's ever made me feel like this.

But I have to keep my distance.

"Is there a reason you're *petting* me?"

"You have a sexy stomach," Rhys blurts, tensing before she shrugs unabashedly against my back. Her persistent fingers curl into my shirt, trying to feel up the muscles underneath again. "Did you know you have a bazillion abs? I swear I counted at least ten of them, and I wasn't even done." Her stream of words aren't awkward this time.

"Is this an oddity for puny human males?" How a woman is ever satisfied by a mortal man is confusing. The ones I witnessed in Rhys's pack were nothing more than overgrown boys hopped up on measly power. They wouldn't survive a single second in the bowels of Hell.

Rhys deserves more than anything they could offer.

Not that I'll be the one to give it to her.

"Ha. Yeah, no." Her head rocks against my back as she shakes it. "I've only seen a ten pack in... uh... movies." The tightness in her voice and the pitch change tells me she's lying.

I cock my head to the side, trying to catch a glimpse of the woman behind me, but all I see is the top of her blonde head.

Aric lifts us high above the ledge Rhys fell from

earlier and lands in a plume of ashy dust. It billows out in a foggy cloud that causes a heavy cough to tremble through Rhys. I swiftly dismount, swinging my leg over the side of the dragon and landing on my feet.

The bastard lowers even further to the ground for Rhys, a courtesy he didn't extend to me.

Reaching up, I catch Rhys as she slips down Aric's gleaming black scales. My hands clasp around her waist, and even though I shouldn't, I pull her against my chest and lower her inch by inch to the ground.

Her breath catches as she feels the hardness waiting for her. I want to hide it from her and bury it in her all at the same time.

Ultimately, I step back from her intoxicating curves.

"Your abs aren't the only thing you have over human men," she whispers under her breath shyly, and my lips actually tug up in one corner.

Rhys's sky blue eyes sparkle, reminding me of the only thing I'll miss about Midgard. Their sky is bright, warm, and free, exactly like Rhys.

"Where have you seen ten packs, Rhys?" I ask her directly, the hard glare of my gaze settling on her. I dare her to tell me a lie.

She laughs, then sobers when she realizes all three of us are staring at her. Latham and Aric easily overheard our conversation earlier with their enhanced hearing, each of them picking up on the easy inflection of the falsehood she spilled.

She should know better after traveling through

three realms together. She can't keep anything from us.

Perhaps that's why she's so refreshing. Sin doesn't taint Rhys the way it does the rest of us.

There's a purity in her that will draw more than just the three of us into her orbit.

Hell is going to dig its claws into Rhys and rip out every pretty little piece of her soul, coating it in thick, inky, sin filled mire.

"You know... romantic comedies... action flicks... Chris Hemsworth..." She rattles on with a blush staining her cheeks that has nothing to do with the heat rising off of Hell's river.

"Porn." Aric smirks as he shifts back to the asshole he always is.

Rhys's eyes grow wide, but the blush deepens until it's nearly red, admitting it without words.

"You watch porn?" Latham asks, interest lighting his eyes like he never expected such a sin from such an innocent girl.

But Rhys isn't innocent.

She's pure goodness.

There's a difference.

She shrugs lightly.

Latham's bewildered eyes widen. "Like... what kind?"

And then even Aric is more than interested in her response.

I have to admit I'm fucking dying to know as well,

but I try to smooth the awkward smile on her beautiful face.

Reality and too many dark memories sink back into me. For some people, sex isn't comfortable or freeing.

And I hate the idea of this conversation making her feel that way.

No one should feel that way.

"That's enough," I rumble in her defense, and Rhys's stunned gaze flicks back to mine. "Sex is natural. However someone finds pleasure isn't your fucking business."

But it was Latham and Aric's business last night.

The same sultry image of her throwing her head back, of her beautiful tits thrusting outward, hard and rosy, fills my mind until I harden myself and scowl at the three of them for dragging me into the conversation I rationally know I walked straight into.

I swallow hard.

No. Rhys isn't innocent at all.

She's a fucking temptress.

A siren calling me to deeper depths I'll surely drown in.

I storm away, heading for the now unguarded bridge to the underworld.

"Makes sense." Aric shrugs as they all trail after me. "She likes to watch as much as she likes being involved."

My teeth grind.

"That's why you liked watching me kiss Aric," Latham muses.

"I'm damn sure it was *me* kissing *you*, pretty boy," Aric counters. "And you fucking liked it."

"What's not to like?" Latham sounds genuinely confused.

"Exactly," Rhys says, all dreamy and content.

Gods. Make it stop.

"Can we focus?" I snap, tiring of the conversation that's heading nowhere good. I'm not in the mood to hear more about their sexual exploits when I'm having enough trouble burying Rhys's moans into the deep recesses of my mind.

Who the fuck am I kidding? If anyone is lying, it's me. I'm buried so far in my fabrications I'm borderline delusional.

Forget Rhys?

Somehow I doubt I'll be able to forget anything about her. Perhaps I won't. Maybe memories of her will be a gift. I'll only pull them out on my darkest days. They'll be a spark in the darkness, a pinprick of light in the onyx nights ahead.

Rhys reminds me of what I used to be. Of what I used to have.

Of everything I'm now denied.

She's the pure embodiment of everything awakening in my tainted soul that I was sure shriveled away long ago.

"So where are we going now?" Rhys practically jogs to keep up with my longer strides, and I slow

marginally. Not enough to show her I care about her wellbeing, but enough so she can walk at a fast clip without falling on her face and landing in the river of fire.

That fucking cat of hers laps up the flames of the river in a bizarre sight I can't stand to look at.

I sigh and keep walking at my casual pace that has the woman at my side running ragged.

I've saved her enough for one day. Deep down, I know that if she can't handle Hell's Gate, she'll never survive what's inside.

I don't want to see her damaged like I am, her light snuffed out by the hardships that plague the desolate realm beyond these gates.

Every bone in my body wants to protect her from what lies ahead, but she signed her fate the day she decided to follow us to Hell.

Not that I wouldn't have dragged her there myself if she refused, but that was before I knew her. Before I witnessed her strength and magic and heart.

I shouldn't care. I shouldn't.

"Torben?" Slender fingers curl around my arm. Her skin is soft and creamy against my golden coloring, darkened from too many years of living in Hell.

"Hmm?" I hum distractedly, solely focused on where she's touching me.

"Are you okay?" Rhys asks genuinely. I almost forgot what it was like to have someone worry about me. It's been so damn long.

It's strange.

"I—" I'm speechless is what I am, but I'm not going to tell her that. Firelight flickers in her blue eyes, warming them until they glow like the golden gates of Asgard.

"I'm fine," I finally manage.

"I've been hearing that word a lot today," Rhys mutters, clearly not believing a word of it. "Aren't you happy to be going home?" She eyes the towering castle in the distance. It juts against the crimson sky like it's giving it a giant middle finger. The impressive stone structure is our last stop before it's too late to turn back.

And it's definitely not a place I've ever attributed to the word home.

I want to tell her to run in the other fucking direction, but my tongue glues itself to the roof of my mouth, refusing to work properly.

"I don't think any of us are all that excited to be back," Aric answers darkly, saving me from my brief mutism.

Rhys skips ahead of us and turns sharply, her pale blonde hair whipping over her shoulder as she stares us down.

"I don't understand." She shakes her head as she says it. "Why not?"

My jaw jumps, and I don't dare look to Aric and Latham.

We have our orders, and they know the punishment for spilling Hela's secrets. None of us

fully know the extent of Hela's plans for Rhys, but she wanted her removed from Midgard for a reason. Her mother was no more than a lure.

"It's Hell, Love." Latham scratches at the back of his neck. "It's pretty different from what you're used to in the Realm of the Living."

She turns in a circle, motioning around her like that part was obvious, and I carefully move her away from the edge of the river gurgling and spitting fire just behind her.

Gods, this girl is never going to survive here without our help.

"We all serve our purpose here," Aric states cryptically in a voice that's dark and dry, lacking his earlier warmth.

Rhys nods, understanding softening her expression, though I know she doesn't truly comprehend. Not yet, anyway, but if she follows us into Hell, she will. That's not a promise, it's a fact.

"The pack was the same. Everyone has a role, some much more glamorous than others." A shiver works down her spine, and I can tell she's thinking about the role she almost had at the hands of the sadistic mate she rejected. "Anything is better than what I walked away from." Resolve straightens her spine, and I want to growl at what we saved her from.

Dead fucker got what was coming to him, if you ask me.

And that's just further proof that my soul is as black as Aric's or Latham's now. There's not one ounce of sympathy in me for the way that asshole died. Anyone who mistreats Rhys will get the same. And that *is* a promise.

"Come on," Latham urges, trying to cover the awkward tension that just infiltrated our group. "We're almost there." Their fingers lock together like an intricate knot and he tugs her after him, heading straight for Hell.

Chapter Twenty-Two

Like a Dog

Rhys

They're not telling me something. I feel it the same way I can feel how much our relationships have changed. I'm not just a job to them anymore, and they're not just the three hot assholes who waltzed into my life and messed it all up.

And if I'm being truly honest, they didn't mess it up at all. I'm not sure I was living until now. I've never felt more alive.

I'm no longer the pack's punch line, nor their punching bag. I think... I think I'm starting to belong somewhere, or at least with someone—three someone's to be precise—and that feels... good. Nearly as good as it was being between Aric and Latham. The pleasure is different, but both kinds are just as addictive.

Aric, Latham, and yes, even Torben have embedded themselves into my heart more than anyone ever has before.

I'm not the same girl I was when they arrived, and I'd like to think these men are different now too.

We mean something to each other. We're a misfit pack now. So why the fuck are they keeping secrets from me?

Latham's fingers tighten on mine, his thumb stroking sure, even sweeps over my skin. It settles the worry swirling through my mind and my heart skips a beat at the crooked smile he offers. I could lick that dimple that pops in his cheek just above the curve of his lips.

Bringing my hand to his mouth, he brushes a sweet kiss over my knuckles in a possessive way that has my ovaries swooning.

It's the perfect distraction from the scorching hot metal bridge we're crossing. The molten iron sears away at the soles of my boots, and I don't dare touch anything for fear of losing flesh. The sizzling river rushes below us, promising death if I lose my balance and fall in. Torben's right at my back like a giant bodyguard. I swear he thinks I'm going to have a ditzy blonde moment and just teeter off the edge and go for a quick flaming hot swim.

I could grumble about it, because so far every time he's had to save me has either been because I was following their directions or for a good cause, but there's something oddly endearing about the giant man worrying about me enough to be on alert.

And I have the feeling he doesn't want me to notice. So I'll play blissfully unaware while silently letting him protect me in that brooding, surly way of his.

"Alright, so far I took on ice giants, survived a kraken, tricked an ogre over a cliff, and rode a dragon—"

"Yeah, you did," Aric adds to that last one. He sounds so cocksure, but honestly, he should be. I clench my thighs just thinking about our time together until I force myself to focus as we step off the end of the bridge and gather there.

"What's next?" Apprehension flits through my stomach like a hummingbird on crack. I get that we're not going to just get to waltz into Hell. One can only hope, but I've never been the lucky type.

But really, what else could there be? I see the castle, it's right there.

My mom is right there.

"I'm not sure I've ever met anyone this eager to cross Hell's gates." Torben's censure cuts through me as easily as a knife through butter.

"I'm not eager to go to Hell," I correct him with a shake of my head. "I'm eager to see my mother."

"Of course you are," Latham soothes. "It's been a long time since you've seen her."

He says it like he doesn't know, and I wonder how much they knew before they were sent to fetch me.

"I've never met her." I swallow carefully and pretend not to feel the sting of those words. The little girl who spent every birthday wishing for her mother is bared to them, that vulnerable part of me wide open for them to see.

I try to cover it, but Torben surprises me by lifting my chin with a large, hooked finger. "There's no shame in missing what you should've had." Mossy green eyes bore intently into mine. It's like he knows just how many stars I wished on, how many nights I lay awake waiting on her, how many hopeless days passed before I finally gave up.

Sure, I wondered about a father from time to time, but it isn't the same. Part of me has always felt like I could hear her calling to me. Like her voice was always burned into the back of hidden memories I just couldn't reach.

And Torben, he understands because he's just as broken as I am.

Our damage breathes between the scant inches separating us.

Just like that, he gives me permission to grieve, and it's the greatest gift I've ever received.

No one tells you it's okay not to be okay. That it's okay to cry, to yell, to feel. To wish on a million stars and be disappointed when none of them come true. It's okay to fall apart sometimes, as long as we find ourselves again in the aftermath. And more importantly, that it's okay to find new happiness.

Mine just happened to come in the shape of three hellish gods I never saw coming.

The way Torben looks at me forms an unbreakable bond, and if nothing else ever develops

between us, we have this trust like I've never felt with anyone in my entire life.

I swallow and the warrior god drops his hand after a prolonged moment. I miss his touch when it's gone and I dip my head, sure it's written all over my face.

Loki mewls, transforming before my eyes in a ball of fire that fizzles out into the form of a small gray house cat. The four of us peer down at the little creature now swaying around my ankles

"Why'd he do that?" Aric asks gruffly.

I shrug, but then the tiny creature prowls toward Aric. It sits down promptly and stares up at the man, waiting.

Latham looks hesitantly toward Aric. The dragon shifter cocks his scarred eyebrow, glaring at the pet like it's a ticking time bomb.

Which I guess he kind of is.

"Why's he looking at you like that?" Latham asks quietly like any wrong move could have them right back on the cat's shit list.

Aric tilts his head this way and that. The cat holds the man's gaze with a poker face I've never seen on my sweet kitten.

"Alright, fine!" Aric throws his hands in the air before slipping his hand into his pocket.

He pulls out the bag. Loki's bag, apparently.

The possessive cat meows as if he's disappointed at the shifter's petty theft.

The bag gets laid out on the ground, and Loki swiftly curls up in the center of it.

"I guess he wants to be carried now." Latham shakes his head at the spoiled brat, while I smile like he's the cutest little cat in the whole wide world.

"Here." Latham waves his hand and procures a fine porcelain water bowl as well as a canteen, pouring some water for Loki before passing it to me with a look that says to finish the rest.

I know they're worried about me. I'm parched, so I don't hesitate. The cool water is refreshing against my heated, dry throat. All this ash can't be good for a person's health.

Then again, when you're immortal, maybe that's not a concern.

Aric takes the bowl and squats down to offer it to Loki. Then he pulls out a piece of dried meat from his pocket, and I'm really starting to wonder just what all he has hoarded away in those jeans. He extends the piece of meat to the cat, and watching this monster of a man take to my pet is the sweetest thing I've ever seen.

The cat sniffs the meat with a disgusted look before sniffing the contents of the bowl. Loki takes a small pretentious sip, but other than that he gets back to his resting.

Aric shakes his head and pockets the dried meat once more.

"I saw the thing drink fire. I don't think we have to worry about keeping it hydrated," Torben grumbles. "The hellcat is useless." Torben's clearly not at all appreciating my cat for the badass he apparently is.

"He's got a damn good bite on him." Aric winces, rubbing absently at the perfectly healed bite mark on his leg. There's not even a scar thanks to his advanced healing, but I have a feeling it's an injury he won't soon forget.

We let my cat rest for a few minutes while I finish the canteen. When we start off again though, Loki quickly pounces out of his bag that he all but demanded from Aric. He stays close to me, not letting me far from his sights. I smile down at my strange little guardian who might forever be a mystery to me.

All the conversation turns to Loki as we trek up the path that leads to the castle, and I know it's an easy way for us to move past the heavy moments we'd been in a few minutes earlier. Loki pads along, taking time to occasionally bat at the rustling blades of grass or pounce on weird-looking insects that are so far removed from the mortal realm it's disconcerting.

When the conversation grows quieter and then stops altogether, I know we're nearing our destination.

Or worse.

I pick up Loki, pet him between his ears, and quickly pop him back into the bag. "Stay there," I warn, and he gives me the most sarcastic look, like he can't believe how our roles have reversed and I'm guarding him.

Either way, I zip the bag shut, leaving just enough space to allow some decent airflow, and move to shoulder the pack before Aric plucks it from my fingers again.

A grateful smile pulls up my lips and then I'm

listening to the guys talk strategy, leaving me completely in the dark as to what the hell is going on as they guide me behind a large boulder on the outskirts of the looming castle.

I peer over it as I listen to them talk about a dog or a wolf or something that guards the gate, just making out the shadowy figure of a sleeping creature. The gates to Hell are a huge iron contraption with intricate scenes embossed in the thick, dark metal. A large chain slinks along the ground like a great fiery snake, attaching to a collar full of spikes that protrude outward in every direction from the beast's enormous neck.

"He looks peaceful," I murmur, not realizing the soft words will halt the conversation flowing around me to silence.

Aric scoffs and a ghost of a smile graces Latham's kissable lips. Torben looks to the heavens like they'll be able to save him, and I prop my hands on my hips.

"The hellhound is chained. Can't we just skirt past him and go through the gate?" It seems like an obvious plan, but it's apparently flawed from the way they're looking at me.

"That chain gives him plenty of leeway," Latham explains.

"And you have to prove your strength and cunning before he'll allow you to pass."

Torben shrugs, not disagreeing with the others. "Garm's strength and ferocity are legendary, plus he has a wicked bite and breath of fire. You won't get within ten feet without being roasted to a crisp for

daring to cross him."

"So what the hell are we supposed to do?" I stare at the beast, still standing by my assessment. "Don't tell me you're going to take him out." For no apparent reason, I have a lot more loyalty to this sleeping beast than I did for the ogre, and I can't stand the idea of him getting hurt. Unlike the guardian of the bridge, the guardian of the gate has no freedom. The chain binds him, digging into his black fur and rubbing him raw where the iron shackles around his neck.

No one should be stuck like that. The wolf inside of me agrees, howling out her feelings on the matter.

She's just as appalled as I am at Garm's treatment.

"No one 'takes out' the guardian of Hell, Love," Aric tells me.

The three of them huddle together like Hell's hottest football team to create a game plan.

"Draw it to the left until the chain is taut. If you keep it distracted, Aric can swoop down from above and singe the fucker before he can roast us," Torben muses.

"Or…" I hold up a finger, chiming in from the cheerleading section they've so obviously put me in. All I need are some pom poms and an outfit with a little skirt that shows off my legs and tits. "Latham could poof in and out, keeping him distracted while we sneak past the gate." It seems like a perfectly plausible option, so I have no clue why they're all staring at me with skeptical, unimpressed expressions.

"I don't go poof." Latham shakes his head, accidentally tossing his hair across his forehead before flicking it away with that sexy head jerk thing guys do.

"You are kind of poofy." Aric smiles that feral cat grin, the wicked, mischievous glint in his golden eyes burning as brightly as the fiery river I'm content to never see again.

"If I am, so are you, you shadow asshole." Latham nudges Aric, the two of them bantering like old women. It warms my heart to see them together like this, but I take the opportunity as they go back to planning to tap Aric on the shoulder.

Distracted, he only gives me half an ear.

"Do you have any more of that dried meat?" I inquire sweetly, and he grunts as he listens to Torben's new plan that involves flaming swords.

He distractedly pulls out a hefty portion of meat and plops it in my palm without so much as a glance my way. Latham nods almost manically when Torben mentions the fiery sword again. I'm fairly sure these men would agree to anything that includes flaming weapons.

If the way to a man's heart is through his stomach, the way to a hellish god's heart is through weaponry.

And sex. Let's not forget the sex.

I hum quietly to myself as I take the hunk of meat and sneak away. It's honestly too easy. They're not even paying attention as my soft, padding footsteps carry me toward the resting beast.

He rouses in his sleep the moment I get close, one large eye popping open as he assesses what disturbed his slumber.

"Hey there, big fella," I coo in that voice that Loki despises but secretly loves. I hold the meat behind my back, easing forward as he lifts his monstrous head, both fiery, glowing red eyes fixated on my slight form. Compared to Garm, I'm a pixie. He's massive, his paws span the entire width of my body.

A deep rumbling growl begins, and I hold out a hand.

"I'm not here to hurt you," I tell him, hoping he'll understand my nonthreatening tone, if not the words themselves. "That looks like it hurts." My heart aches at the bleeding skin I spy chafing below the metal collar. No living being should ever be chained up, their freedom stripped to ribbons.

Anger curls in my stomach.

"Rhys!" Torben barks as they finally realize I'm not standing around waiting for them.

Maybe it's stupid, but I don't want anyone else to hurt this guy.

The beast stands, towering far above my head, and I hear the loud cursing suffuse the air behind me.

"Easy." I take a step back, realizing that the beastly hellhound they call Garm could reach me in one bound. A single bite from those powerful jaws, and I'd be a goner. There wouldn't be enough of me left to bury six feet under.

The hound prowls forward, his massive paw shaking the ground until I'm stumbling around like a drunk person on Mardi Gras.

This close, I can see all the scars and injuries that

line his matted fur from previous battles he's fought or had to defend himself against.

"I don't want them to have to hurt you," I tell him honestly. "Don't do this." Command fills my tone as I straighten my shoulders. My feet slide backward in the ashy dirt, one smooth footfall at a time as the hound stalks closer, hunting his easy prey.

He bares his teeth at me and lunges. I dart to the right, narrowly escaping the crash of jaws and gnashing of teeth as he growls and attacks.

The swipe of his big paw catches the edge of my arm as I try to duck out of his reach. Blood trickles out of the slashing wounds, but my wolf presses close, pushing her healing abilities into the injury until it begins knitting together.

Despite being hurt, I don't want to retaliate the way my entourage of men rushing forward want to do.

I turn and hold my hands up at the three of them, searing them with an angry glare that slows their steps instantly.

"It's not his fault this is what he's trained to do." The reprimand pulls Latham up short, his expression bleeding from furious to sheepish as he realizes what I say is right. "This is all he knows. Violence. Blood. Pain."

I whirl, and the hound lowers his stance, ready to attack once more from where he spun around, never giving me his back. Another learned behavior. I know that feeling.

And my heart wins out. My magic unfurls. The power inside me builds until I push it toward Garm.

I let my shift wash over me, tearing at my limbs and ripping apart my joints in a scream-riddled moment of pain. The food in my hand falls to the ground. My four paws dig into the dirt as I stretch, pick up the dried meat, and walk slowly toward the hellhound.

His head tilts curiously at my white wolf.

Warm magic is a steady stream between us as I lope closer, taking it as a good sign that he's not attacking.

Setting the meat down in front of him, I nudge it with my nose. In comparison to Garm's size, it's nothing more than a kibble, but I doubt anyone has brought him anything this fresh in a long time, unless you count anyone he gets to rip apart and snack on.

He bares his teeth, sneering at the gift like it's poisoned.

I cock my head, staring. Then I lower my snout and take a tentative bite of the offering.

The growling stops, and the wolf tilts his head like I just did, staring at me with confusion.

I nudge the meat again, and this time he rakes it closer with a powerful paw.

Dipping low, he sniffs it, then licks it, then dives in, tearing it apart in a second flat, leaving no trace of it behind.

Shifting back, I stand before the beast fully naked, uncaring about my nudity. My chin lifts high, my gaze matching his with respect and care. A few steps and I'm able to dig my hand into his matted fur.

"I wish I could brush this for you. It'd hurt more than feel good right now, but every girl knows if you don't brush away the knots, they just get worse. I bet no one has taken any time to groom you since you were born, have they?" My palm runs over the soft fur, taking in the numerous dips and scars and roughened skin beneath. This poor creature has been through hell for a being that lives just outside of it.

I send another wave of that mysterious power in my veins, and the hellhound lies down at my feet. His big eyes look up at me and my whole fucking heart melts for him.

As my nails dig behind his ears and around his neck, he rolls over fully for me to get his belly too.

"Aww." I smile down at the good boy.

"The fuck?" Aric whispers, inching closer now that I've tamed the big bad wolf.

"Have you ever seen anything like this?" Latham asks.

"I've been through this gate a few times. I won't lie, I'm responsible for a few of those scars. And I've never seen him act like this before." Torben scratches his blond beard in astonishment. "We're sure the meat wasn't poisoned with something?" He swings his attention to Aric.

"If it was poisoned, I'd be getting fucking belly rubs right now too, dammit."

"He just needed a little love," I say, reaching up to scratch behind Garm's ear again. He leans his head into me, licking his chops as he cranes his neck to get a better angle on my ministrations.

"Doesn't everyone?" Aric grins. He sighs and runs a hand down his face. The day clings to us all, and once again Latham hands me another bundle of conjured clothing. I step back from the sweet hound, his lazy gaze following me. I stagger as I step into the black pants and pull on the crop top and boots. The neckline is high, but the entire expanse of my stomach is on display, keeping it modest and yet extremely sexy simultaneously. A feat most girls try to accomplish daily. Latham just gets it. I appreciate him in a way I can't put into words. I've never had someone take care of me like he does.

I don't even think he realizes it. He just gives. Freely.

"What were you thinking?" Torben questions harshly when I'm finally dressed. He was trying to be respectful and keep his eyes off my goodies, but now that I'm decent he doesn't hold back. His attention is wandering across my curves and stomach even as he grumbles on. "That was reckless and irresponsible."

"You said one needed to be cunning to be granted entrance," I snipe back, because really… what can I say? He's kind of right. Kind of. I shrug anyway. "You're welcome." I grin like my plan couldn't have gotten me killed for my stupidity rather than my cleverness. "He's just a puppy."

"An evil hell pup who eats people like they're hors d'oeuvres," Aric adds.

"He almost ate you," Latham obligingly points out to me.

"He was just hangry."

All three men raise their brows at the unfamiliar word. Honestly, if it's not already added to the dictionary, it should be. It embodies the feeling perfectly.

"You got lucky," Torben grumbles, trying to get the last word.

I'm too competitive for that shit. "You catch more flies with honey than vinegar."

"That makes no fucking sense!" he bites out, trying to roll that saying around in his head. I can see the gears turning as he mulls it over. "Why would you want to catch fucking flies?" he finally says, and I giggle at the brute of a man.

At my side, Garm licks my hand and whines, asking for more food.

Aric empties his pockets for the beast before I even have to ask. I offer the last of our rations to the puppy, and he gobbles them up quickly.

There's no more protest as we move past him and knock on the gate that leads to Hell. The loud clanging of fist to metal echoes into the crimson sky above. It takes a few long minutes. They tick by with the heavy pounding of my heart.

I don't glance around. I don't look questioningly to Latham like I want to. I try my best to act like I'm not scared shitless that I came all this way and nearly died so, so many times just to be denied at the door.

Out of thin air, a figure appears.

I flinch but hold my ground.

The black cloth of the person's cloak drags in the

dirt, and yet none of it stains the pure onyx fabric. Not an inch of their features or hands can be seen. Darkness clings to whatever lies beneath the hooded cloak.

The shrouded figure answers the door, swinging it open on a cry of hinges before ushering us inside.

"This way," a woman's voice says, a ghostly air lingering along her words. I take a step, but she speaks once more. "No pets allowed."

I halt instantly, my gaze falling on the small gray cat at my feet. My stomach drops at the thought of leaving a house cat in the depths of Hell.

Until Loki bursts into fucking flames. The fiery hellcat languidly strides toward Garm. Loki takes a seat in the curve of the hound's resting body and watches me intently.

He and I came here together, both of us trying to find where we truly belong. Our journey is over though. My sweet lifelong friend can't come along with me any further. This is where I leave him. It's possibly where he's belonged all along.

Just like me.

My heart dips at that thought, but seeing him side by side with Garm feels safe.

I smile sadly at the enormous flaming cat who will forever be my pet and guardian. His head dips with a curt nod, a strangely knowing nod.

And I turn away with a sense of peace.

The three men follow me closely on all sides. I swallow hard and stride forward with my head held high.

With a backward glance, I make a silent promise that I'll find a way to help Garm find freedom, one way or another. No one—not even this beast—deserves to be treated like a dog, or worse, like a possession to be abused.

I know all too well about being a victim of circumstance.

Garm and I are more alike than anyone realizes.

And now, I'm walking into his prison.

With my head held high.

Chapter Twenty-Three

The DGE

Rhys

The woman's thick black cloak covers her from head to toe, but hints of white bone now sneak out with the swishing of her hemline as she leads us into the castle.

What is she?

Latham steps closer to me when she guides us down a shadowy hall. His arm brushes mine as we walk side by side, and somehow, the meager amount of space between us keeps getting smaller, as if he wants to just wrap me up entirely in his arms to shield me from what's to come.

When we turn down the first hall at the entrance of the metallic castle, the darkness becomes dense and heavy around us. I can hear her footfalls ahead of me and the pairs of solid steps of the men behind me, but I can't see a single thing.

And then I hear it.

A scream like flesh being torn from the bone little by little claws across the walls and scurries around us, over and over again. Thousands of them sing out in a horrific symphony of agony. My spine tenses hard, my steps falter, but I never stop walking. I keep going while the screams scratch like nails dragging over the brick floors.

A warm arm slips around my waist, and Latham pulls me closer to his side. It's the simplest gesture shared in the dark.

The pounding of my heart calms. Though I know he's keeping secrets, I think I trust him.

It's a terrifying thought in the most terrifying setting, but it's true.

"What is this place?" I whisper quietly to him. "I thought we were going to be in Hell once we passed the gates." This certainly doesn't look like anything I expected.

Not a single flame of hellfire shoots up from the floors here. No men hang on racks of torment. No men with pitchforks.

It all has a rather... haunted house feeling.

Except much, much more sinister.

"'Tis the Hall of Misery," the woman answers for him, her voice nothing more than an airy breath.

I swallow hard as I try to imagine what that means.

"After death, some require punishment. For example, a lifetime of unending famine. A pain of the body literally eating itself to try to find nutrients. Just

something to remind them of any wrong doings." Her hollow voice quiets, the screams fade, and light illuminates a large open room up ahead. "Here we are," she says, and as she turns to nod to us, the light shines across her, showing the features just beneath her thick hood.

A shiver spider walks down my arms at the sight of her. Skin the color of rotting fish clings to the hard bones of her skull just beneath. One eye socket is empty and dark, while the other has the remnants of an eyeball hanging down near the divot of her face where her nose should be.

My throat constricts as she passes me by, leaving us here in the safety of the light.

"Safe travels," she whispers to each of us with a bow.

I'm still pressed tightly into Latham's side. Aric steps forward with a glance at how intimately his friend holds me. He looks like he wishes it was him standing next to me, but as is his way, he says nothing. He lowers his head instead.

Someday, after all of this passes—*if* all of this passes—I might have a hard choice to make. A choice that could cost friendships.

And I won't ruin their friendship.

My heart convulses, and I try not to think about losing them. Not right now anyway.

Strange music meets my ears, and I peer up at the room. My brows lower as I take in the weirdest thing I've seen yet in this realm.

The intense fluorescent brightness of the room falls across Aric's inky tattoos, making him look more like the relentless protector I've come to know him to be.

"Have you been here before?" the shifter asks Latham and Torben.

Latham shakes his head slowly. "I was born into the Realm of Hell. And the people I bring here are runaways. Already Hell bound."

"Same here," Aric says, his gaze passing over the bizarre room with a hard line tensing his brow.

Torben stays quiet though. Latham releases me as we all turn to look back at the man who hasn't answered.

"Yeah," is all he utters.

"Care to enlighten us?" Aric shoves his arms across his solid chest.

The silence that slips in where Torben's explanation should be leaves an unsettling restlessness inside me. This is bad. If a warrior of Hell doesn't want to talk about how dark this part of Hell is, it has to be tortuous. Unimaginable horrors slice apart my thoughts with blood and gore.

The moment I turn back around to assess the wide-open span of the room, a busy chatter of noise falls across the music that I've only ever heard in elevators in the human world. The open space springs to life with desks of workers all typing furiously. And fax machines. I've never seen so many fax machines in all my life.

I didn't think people used them any more since the age of email. It'd be quicker to send a message by raven, to be honest.

A digital dial up of an error rings louder and louder through the room, assaulting my ears and thought processes as I try to take it all in. It's all noise layered on top of other noise.

"Take a number, please," a woman calls out like an angry crow.

I glance at Torben. The line between his brows is so deep it looks like his head might split wide open as he rubs the spot tenderly.

"What is this place?" I ask in a hushed tone, conspiracy edging into my voice. Aliens and Bigfoot and the proper spelling of the Berenstain Bears all have to be tied together with this shit, right?

Torben shakes his head slowly like it pains him to remember.

"It's the DGE: The Department of Good and Evil." His words are a rumble of grunted syllables, but his gaze narrows on the desk straight ahead of us.

"I said take a number!" the woman squawks at us.

"Fucking hellhole," Torben grumbles before jerking a little tag of paper off of a machine and plopping down in one of the many chairs that line the wall to our right. He practically dwarfs the small seat.

I quietly lower myself into the chair next to him. The plastic bites into my thighs, and an older woman at my side holds a little slip of paper in her fingers as well.

"How long have you been waiting?" I whisper to her as I shift in the hard chair.

I push my hair back to fully look at her. Her mouth hangs wide open. An empty stare straight ahead consumes her gaze. A buzzing sound flits in just as a small black fly lands on her lower lip.

And she still doesn't move.

"She's dead, Love," Aric tells me casually before pushing harshly at the ash brown hair atop his head and spinning in an astounded circle to fully take in the dozens of workers typing furiously.

But ultimately... doing nothing. And helping no one.

"Excuse me!" he barks out so loudly the small blonde woman at the desk closest to us nearly jumps out of her seat.

"Yes?" she answers politely.

"Could you assist us? Get us the hell out of this fuckin' section of Hell, by chance?" His manic gaze pins her in place, and she shakes her head, her long hair quaking as she does.

"I'm not actually qualified. Karen is the lead processor of souls. Not me." She shrugs her delicate shoulders, and I note the fearful glance she tosses toward the woman at the desk straight ahead.

"Oh, come on," Aric whispers rather sweetly, and the tilt of his half smile is enough to make her breath fall hard from her lips.

I fucking know it. When that deadly man smiles, my ovaries take on a heartbeat of their own. They take on a brain of their own too. And I'm left stupid and pussy pulsing while he gets anything his little black heart desires.

And he knows he has that effect on women.

"Please?" he asks with big demonic puppy dog eyes.

"For god's sake," Torben mutters with a hard shake of his head.

"I-I guess I could do it for you," the woman answers in a dazed, far-off voice.

"Thank you." He looks quickly down at her golden name plate. "Thank you, Asta."

The four of us gather around her little black desk while she shuffles through a filing cabinet. When her old brown chair spins back around, she's holding a clipboard, her pen already hovering over the page.

"Let's see. We'll start with a basic questionnaire. In the last three years," she says, and my stomach suddenly twists.

What if I don't know the answers? What if we don't pass? Shit, why am I always so unprepared for exams like this?

"In the last three years, have you filed taxes?" She lifts her innocent face up to the four of us, and I blink at the randomness of her words.

Oh. That's not so bad. My lips part to answer, but someone else speaks up first.

"What the fuck are taxes?" Latham answers.

And she nods.

"Mmm. I see." Her pen scratches over the paper

while Latham, Torben, and Aric whisper together about king's gold and village dues.

"Let's try something new," she carries on, and I close my mouth, unsure now if my answer is needed.

Aric nods, staring at her like he's ready to speed answer her questions and be announced the winner of Who Wants to get the Fuck Outta Hell?

"Say you're at a traffic light. The signal turns green, but the vehicle ahead of you does not move." She looks up at us. "What do you do?"

My lips part hesitantly but Aric is just too ready. "I fuckin' skin him, eat his flesh, and devour his bones for wasting my fuckin' time."

What. The. Fuck?

My mouth falls open as I stare at him.

Torben's brows lift and he scratches lightly at his beard, but ultimately he nods, pleased with that answer.

"Mm-hmm." The woman makes a little mark with another quick scribble of her pen.

"Say someone leaps into a river, but they can't swim. Would you risk your life to save theirs?" She looks at us one by one.

"Why did they get in a river if they can't swim?" Latham whispers quietly.

"Why would I risk my life when this asshole might just dive back in?" Torben adds.

"Seems like a setup." Aric looks to the others and they both nod. "Someone wants us dead." More agreeing nods.

Asta jots all of those answers down, but I feel like we're failing an exam on basic human decency. What the fuck kind of lunatic pack did I team up with here?

"I—" The woman stops writing the moment I make a single noise. "I-I'm a stronger swimmer. I could help the person in the river."

Her empty expression lingers on me for several beats while Torben shakes his head with disappointment in my response. "People like that will get you killed, princess," he murmurs under his breath.

"I see," she says as she flips the page and writes something I can't see.

"What's your name?" she asks without looking up from her notes.

"Rhys. Rhys Love."

With another quick note she looks directly up at me.

"Miss Love, if the world were to end in a... fairly horrific way, but you could stop it, you could save humanity" —her big brown eyes gleam as she gazes intently at me— "would you sacrifice yourself to save everyone else?"

"No." Aric drops that answer like it's final and nothing more will be said about it.

I arch an annoyed eyebrow at the hellacious man, but consider the question for myself.

"I—"

"No," he growls once more.

"She asked me," I snap under my breath.

"And I'm saying no. In no hypothetical or real way

251

would I allow you to fuckin' dive into a river after some swimless fuck, let alone give your life to save a society of people who have never showed you an ounce of fucking kindness!" His big palm slams flat on the woman's desk and she flinches on impact.

But I don't look away from him for a second.

"Bea did," I whisper.

The image of her hurt expression during the Dark Moon is fresh in my mind, and it's honestly the main focus as I consider giving my life for the world.

I'd save her. Even Mary. Maybe even fucking Calvin. I'd save them all if I could. Because my small, insignificant life isn't comparable to the human race as a whole.

There are good people out there, even if I never experienced much kindness or love myself. I felt it in the way the shyest boy in our class loved Bea. The way he looked at her when she didn't notice. The way he kissed her when he knew he couldn't keep her. I felt it with every washing wave of my magic that I gave out, time and time again.

I felt love. It was just never mine.

And that's enough to know my answer.

"I'd give my life for theirs," I say firmly, giving Asta my final answer.

Torben shakes his head like I'm the most foolish woman he's ever kidnapped.

Aric looks furious. The hard set of his jaw tells me he wants to shift so damn bad it must hurt.

While Latham… Latham just peers at me with big

shining eyes. He says nothing. He offers no judgment. But something in the way he looks at me makes me feel his hurt.

I don't understand it at all.

Maybe I'll never understand these three psychotic men.

"Well then…" Asta fills in another line on the clipboard before flipping to the front page once more and checking a few tiny boxes at the bottom.

I lean into the hard edge of the desk to steal a peek.

Visitor One: *Hell Bound*
Visitor Two: *Hell Bound*
Visitor Three: *Hell Bound*
Visitor Four, Rhys Love: *Other*

"You three can join me right this way." She motions to the men as she strides with paperwork in hand toward a little gray door at the back of the room. A square sign is positioned just above it and in glowing red letters it reads: HELL.

"Um…" I tilt my head to the side to try to understand what in the literal hell is happening right now.

"I'll be right with you, Miss Love," Asta says with an office-like smile plastered on her pretty face. Elevator music accompanies her every step while it just drills through the confusion in my pounding skull. Still, she heads toward the apparent entrance to Hell.

The men next to me don't make a single move to follow her.

Her palm presses to the gray door and it swings open effortlessly with dry cold air whisking in. Through the door, a rocky cavern of space is seen. Shadows cling to the depths here and there, but no fiery flames of Hell are seen, so I guess that's a good sign.

What isn't, is that I'm not going there.

I've come all this way, I've fought and killed to be here. To finally see her.

Just to be rejected at the door.

"Asta, either submit your visitors or close the door. You know I hate a cold draft!" the woman, Karen, snarls while tightening her red cardigan around herself.

"What the fuck are we supposed to do?" Aric steps closer to me while searching Torben's face for an answer.

"I don't know. We could... go in. Inform Hela what happened and come back for Rhys." Torben doesn't look at me while he plans what to do with me like I'm an old lamp that's taking up too much space.

Just put me in storage. That's basically his plan for the dusty old lamp.

"We're not leaving her," Aric growls.

"You got a better idea?" Torben tosses back at the shifter.

Their bickering turns into a more incessant sound than the grating fax error that's ringing louder by the

second. Anxiety prickles in my chest like a stabbing I can't ignore.

Latham watches me in silence.

No one offers a real solution.

There's nothing.

Nothing we can do.

And then... I see her.

A woman with pale blonde hair tied back steps in front of the door. Her face is so much thinner than the memory that's suddenly flooding into my mind. But her soft blue eyes... they're just like mine.

"You are love," she coos, *tucking in warm blankets all around me.*

"You are love," she *whispers into my hair as she braids back the soft blonde locks.*

"You are love," she *says with tears streaming down her face while she hugs me so tightly the fear in my chest presses harder.*

And then darkness consumes my memories.

There are no more.

"Mom," I whisper among the chaos of angry words and shuffling papers and terrible ringing errors.

Then I'm running. I sprint like a wolf about to shift. It all passes by in a blur of settings. Papers flit to the ground all around my feet. My knee bends, my boot rattles Karen's desk, and I kick off of her keyboard with a clatter of keys in my wake.

Yells can be heard just behind me. It's all alive with thunderous noise that I can barely hear.

Because in the next instant, I leap past Asta,

through the door to Hell, and into my mother's arms.

Chapter Twenty-Four

Welcome Home

Rhys

Her hands tremble but hold me firmly against her thin frame. Long hair curtains over my face as I clench my eyes and inhale her scent so hard that a flood of memories wash into my mind. The ashen smell of honey caresses each and every one of them.

"Mom," I whisper on a cutting breath.

She shakes her head against me and holds on to me like she's afraid I might disappear.

"You shouldn't have come here." Her voice wavers and the tears that soak her cheeks seep into her breathy confession. Her arms tighten around me, belying her words as she refuses to let me go.

An emotion I don't understand—and don't know if I ever will—comes over me: I missed her. I missed her and I didn't even know I missed her until I had her.

My fingers dig into my mother's thin brown shirt, and the sensation that I'm being watched tingles through me. My gaze lifts, and the kindest eyes I've ever known peer into mine. Latham's happiness shines in the depths of those frost-kissed pools. But he wears no smile. That aloof amusement isn't in his handsome features now. In the shadows of the cavernous room, he looks haunted. More tragically beautiful than ever before.

Sad. Fuck, he looks sad.

I pull away from my mother just slightly, and the moment I do, a man with pale features and even paler, white blond hair saunters up to Latham, Aric, and Torben. The man's smile reveals sharp white teeth. Latham's jaw twitches as he glares up at the strange man.

"Enjoy your freedom?" he asks in a slithering tone with that large, creepy smile stretching further across his face.

His hands lift and come down fast and hard. Metal clanks loudly, and Latham falls to his knees. Sparks fly from his wrists as shining black chains link one hand to the other.

My round, wide eyes stare at the horrible scene, my protests clawing their way up my throat. My heart thunders, my wolf snarls, and I'm in that asshole's face in an instant.

"What the fuck are you doing to him?" I stand firmly within the small space between the eerie man

and Latham. The beast inside of me presses to get out with gnashing teeth and snarling lips, but a pressure fights back against it. It feels heavy. Contained. Some form of magic is restraining the animal inside of me, and it only sends more molten hot anger lashing through my chest.

The man's smile turns into a wicked snarl as he lowers his head and runs his nose from my collarbone to my ear.

My skin crawls with the feeling of skittering cockroaches everywhere he dares to touch me.

"Well, aren't you pretty?" he hisses against my flesh, and the rise of vomit scalds my throat.

A warm palm slides around my arm, and Aric slips me behind him as he steps forward with his head held high.

"Don't ever fucking touch her again if you want to keep your fucking tongue, Serpan," he grits out from tightly clenched teeth. His wild, fiery eyes burn into the other man's silver orbs, promising wicked torture before death.

That smile eats up the sharpness of the stranger's features.

"Know your place," the slender man hisses.

Latham's head is bowed, and all I can see is the sharp angle of his jaw as it pulses with rage. I turn to Torben, and there's shame in green eyes. He can't even look at me.

"Fucking fix this!" I shove at his broad chest, but he only exhales a heavy breath, and everything feels like it's fucking falling apart all around me.

"Let's go, pets." A flash of fiery embers burn around Serpan's long fingers. He flings that magic at Aric, and an iron collar falls heavily against the dragon shifter's throat.

My fingers tangle with Aric's, and he squeezes hard before trailing after the asshole like all of this is fucking normal. His hand falls away as he looks back at me just once.

And then my composure fucking shatters.

I'm not that quiet girl anymore. I don't need my wolf to nudge me into sticking up for myself or my friends.

Her rage and mine are now one and the same.

And it all comes lashing out.

My boots echo over the rocky ground furiously. I shoulder past Aric and Latham. My knees bend and I leap into the shadows. My chest collides with a bony spine, and the man crumples beneath me.

"Get—get off of me!" Serpan grunts, but my arm is already fully around his scrawny neck.

"How fucking dare you?" I growl into his ear as I tighten my hold.

Hands claw at my arms, voices call out to me with urgency and warning. A choking noise gargles from Serpan's thin lips, but I refuse to stop.

I'm sick and tired of people tormenting me, hating me, hurting me, and I won't stand for a single second to see it happen to the people I care about. They have to learn that you can't kick someone down without

karma rising up with a vengeance.

And I'm going to make sure this fucker learns.

Sharp nails sink into my throat. The grip tightens, and then I'm hauled backward. A woman with long, inky black hair appears, and her hand tenses hard around my throat as she studies me with a tilt of her head. Big sapphire blue eyes shine into mine as a ghost of a smile kisses her black painted lips.

"You're smaller than I thought you'd be." She lifts my feet off the ground as if she's weighing me as she strangles me. My boots kick and scrape over the rocks, but I can't quite reach.

I can't breathe.

My fingers hold onto hers as if I can stop the pressure she's pressing into my windpipe. My wolf growls and then whines a low, tragic sound.

She still can't get out. She can't help me.

My nails sink into the flesh of her wrists even harder at that thought, and I claw at her.

"Strong though," she adds with curiosity gleaming in her eyes.

Her attention flits to the right and she seems to remember something then. "Serpan, take Latham to his cage. And escort our favorite flesh-eating dragon to his isolation."

My kicking turns violent then. More for vengeance than survival. My boot meets her shin, but she doesn't even flinch. She doesn't notice me at all until she drifts her gaze back to mine.

"Yes, you'll do just fine here," she says sweetly as

261

black spots consume my vision. "You're so very much like your mother." She shakes her head slowly, my lungs burning with a striking pain. "I hate your mother, but she's learned her place." She beams at me as my hands lower before falling limply to my sides. A low growl emits from behind me, so low I question if I truly heard it as my eyes close little by little. "Soon, you will too."

The darkness in the room creeps in like a heavy blanket ready to suffocate me in my sleep.

She releases me, and a slick cracking sound rattles my skull. Her faint words circle in my mind over and over as the world slips away entirely.

"What a pathetic Hell goddess you turned out to be."

Goddess. Goddess. Goddess.

The End

Hell Kissed

The Rejected Realms Series continues! Book two, Fire Kissed is now available!

A.K. Koonce & Harper Wylde

Also by A. K. Koonce

Reverse Harem Books

The To Tame a Shifter Series

Taming

Claiming

Maiming

Sustaining

Reigning

The Monsters and Miseries Series

Hellish Fae

Sinless Demons

A. K. Koonce & Harper Wylde

Spiteful Creatures

The Villainous Wonderland Series

Into the Madness

Within the Wonder

Under the Lies

Origins of the Six

Academy of Six

Control of Five

Destruction of Two

Wrath of One

The Hopeless Series

Hopeless Magic

Hell Kissed

Hopeless Kingdom

Hopeless Realm

Hopeless Sacrifice

The Secrets of Shifters

The Darkest Wolves

The Sweetest Lies

The Royal Harem Series

The Hundred Year Curse

The Curse of the Sea

The Legend of the Cursed Princess

The Severed Souls Series

Darkness Rising

A. K. Koonce & Harper Wylde

Darkness Consuming

Darkness Colliding

The Huntress Series

An Assassin's Death

An Assassin's Deception

An Assassin's Destiny

Dr. Hyde's Prison for the Rare

Escaping Hallow Hill Academy

Surviving Hallow Hill Academy

Paranormal Romance Books

The Cursed Kingdoms Series

Hell Kissed

The Cruel Fae King

The Cursed Fae King

The Crowned Fae Queen

The Twisted Crown Series

The Shadow Fae

The Iron Fae

The Lost Fae

The Midnight Monsters Series

Fate of the Hybrid, Prequel

To Save a Vampire, Book one

To Love a Vampire, Book two

To Kill a Vampire, Book three

A.K. Koonce & Harper Wylde

<u>Stand Alone Contemporary Romance</u>

Hate Me Like You Do

Also By Harper Wylde

The Phoenix Rising Series

Born of Embers

Hidden in Smoke

Spark of Intent

Forged in Flames

Blaze of Wrath

Changed by Fire

Beauty From Ashes

Glimmer of Cinders

The Veil Keeper Series

A.K. Koonce & Harper Wylde

Shadow Touched

Blood Bound

Tethered Magick

Rising Darkness

The Huntress Series

An Assassin's Death

An Assassin's Deception

An Assassin's Destiny

About A. K. Koonce

A.K. Koonce is a USA Today bestselling author. She's a mom by day and a fantasy and paranormal romance writer by night. She keeps her fantastical stories in her mind on an endless loop while she tries her best to focus on her actual life and not that of the spectacular, but demanding, fictional characters who always fill her thoughts.

A.K. Koonce & Harper Wylde

About Harper Wylde

Harper Wylde is an international bestselling author who lives in the countryside of Pennsylvania. As a wife and a mother of two young children, she spends her days chasing after little people and making crazy notes about story ideas all over her home. As a serial entrepreneur, Harper also dabbles in photography and graphic design...but has found that her favorite occupation is the one she's doing now—writing fantasy and paranormal romance. She loves coffee, cooking, chocolate covered pretzels, and characters with hidden strength and endearing flaws! To connect with Harper, follow her on Facebook where you can join her author group called The Wylde Side and stay up to date on sneak previews, teasers, and new releases!